Did Dinosaurs Snore?

wo metres tall and with an impressively bushy
Philip Ardagh is not only very large and very
e's also become a familiar face – and what a face
ook festivals throughout England, Scotland and

sometimes mistaken for a caveman, he'd be the
point out that neither he nor any other human
is ever come face-to-face with a living, breathing
ir... but that doesn't stop him knowing a great
out them.

t as writing non-fiction, Philip Ardagh is also the
of *Awful End*, a very funny and exciting
1's adventure story – also published by Faber &
but there aren't any dinosaurs in it – not even a

Other books by Philip Ardagh
published by Faber & Faber

Non-fiction

THE HIEROGLYPHS HANDBOOK
Teach Yourself Ancient Egyptian

'If you've ever wanted to read ancient Egyptian, there's
no better way to start than with this.'
PHILIP PULLMAN, *The Guardian*

THE ARCHAEOLOGISTS' HANDBOOK
The Insiders' Guide to Digging Up The Past
(Published 2002)

Fiction

AWFUL END
The Eddie Dicken Trilogy, Book One
'[A] scrumptious cross between Dickens and Monty
Python... Brilliant'
LYN GARDNER, *The Guardian*

'It would be a sad spirit that didn't find this
book hilarious.'
LUCY JAMES, *The Financial Times*

Did Dinosaurs Snore?

QUESTIONS ABOUT DINOSAURS ANSWERED

PHILIP ARDAGH

ILLUSTRATED BY THE MALTINGS
CARTOONS BY MARK DAVIS

ff

faber and faber

First published in 2001
by Faber and Faber Limited
3 Queen Square, London WC1N 3AU

Designed by Mackerel
Printed in Italy

© Philip Ardagh, 2001

Philip Ardagh is hereby identified as author
of this work in accordance with Section 77
of the Copyright, Designs and Patents Act 1988

A CIP record for this book
is available from the British Library

ISBN 0-571-20653-0

2 4 6 8 10 9 7 5 3 1

CONTENTS

Any complicated words and phrases are explained in the Glossary.

For Cordelia Lynn
and Maureen Coffey,
who've been waiting for a dedication for
about 65 million years.

WHAT ON EARTH'S GOING ON IN THIS BOOK?

With the exception of a section on (nearly) everyone's favourite dinosaur, *Tyrannosaurus rex*, the questions and answers in this book haven't been grouped together in any special order, other than to make it a jolly good read. This means that the dinosaur enthusiast can sit down and enter the Age of the Dinosaurs without having any idea what tricky question may be tackled next.

After every ten questions and answers, there's a QUICK QUIZ to see whether you've remembered what's gone before and, as the book goes on, you might be asked about something which was explained twenty, thirty or more answers ago.

The QUICK QUIZ ANSWERS are on page 127 and, if you've a particular question – about the tallest, fastest, or heaviest dinosaur, for example – check the INDEX on page 128 for page numbers.

A MESSAGE FROM THE AUTHOR

Dinosaurs may have been dead for over 65 million years, but they've been haunting me 24 hours a day every day, ever since I agreed to write this book. They're always there in the back of the mind, either harmlessly chewing vegetation or ruthlessly sinking their jaws and claws into each other. There's no escaping them. They're in the bath. They're on the bus. They're tucked up in bed. It's dinosaurs, dinosaurs, dinosaurs everywhere.

When friends, family or anyone I meet finds out that I'm writing a book with $100^1/_2$ answers to tricky questions about dinosaurs – without fail – they all come up with at least one question of their own. Some are easy to answer. Some of the same questions come up again and again. Others are fiendishly clever questions that send me scuttling back to my cave for a good think.

My thanks to everyone who asked the questions. There must have been more than $100^1/_2$ of you. Thanks also to Héloïse Coffey who was always on hand with calming words and to Dr Angela Milner, Head of the Fossil Vertebrates & Anthropology Division at the Natural History Museum, London, who was there with professional comments and advice when I needed her. (If there are any mistakes, however, they are mine.) Finally, I'd like to thank my editor Suzy Jenvey too. A huge fan of dinosaurs herself, she has even been mistaken for one at parties.

PHILIP ARDAGH
LONDON
2001

 'Were dinosaurs the first animals on Earth?'

No, not by a long way. Life on Earth probably began about 4,500 *million* years ago and, for the first 3,950 million or so of those years, the only living things were very simple forms such as algae – the green sludge in water – or bacteria... Then, about 550 million years ago, came the 'Cambrian explosion' when, in a time of prehistory (before writing) called the Cambrian Period, hundreds of new types of animals appeared. Many died out. Others still have descendants in modern creatures such as molluscs (snails, slugs, clams), and the first tiny animals with backbones. So, before dinosaurs there were fish, insects, amphibians (animals which live in and out of water, such as frogs today) and reptiles. The first dinosaurs appeared about 230 million years ago. (see page 108)

'Why was the park in *Jurassic Park* called Jurassic Park?'

In Steven Spielberg's film about a dinosaur park, based on the book by Michael Crichton, it's called Jurassic because

Jurassic is one of the time periods within the Mesozoic Era, the era when dinosaurs ruled the Earth. The Mesozoic Era is divided into three periods: Triassic (248 million years ago to 205 million years ago), Jurassic (205 million years ago to 142 million years ago) and Cretaceous (142 million years to 65 million years ago). *Tyrannosaurus rex*, which is probably the most famous of all dinosaurs, comes from the Cretaceous rather than the Jurassic Period. By the way, the Mesozoic Era means 'the middle era'. Before it came the Palaeozoic Era and after it came the Cenozoic Era, which we're all living in now. The Jurassic Period was the age of the really big dinosaurs, with herd after herd of plant-eaters moving across the plains, eating all those juicy treetops.

TIMELINE

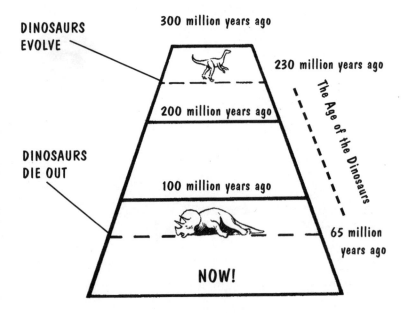

DID YOU KNOW?

The first dinosaurs appeared during the Triassic Period. These included the meat-eating *Herrerasaurus* and *Eoraptor* and the plant-eating *Coelophysis*, and *Melanorosaurus*. They shared the planet with other creatures which had been around for MILLIONS of years.

THE AGE OF THE DINOSAURS
THE MESOZOIC ERA

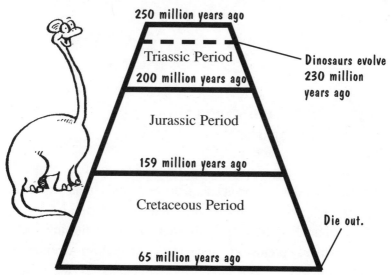

250 million years ago

Triassic Period

Dinosaurs evolve 230 million years ago

200 million years ago

Jurassic Period

159 million years ago

Cretaceous Period

Die out.

65 million years ago

13

3 'Were all dinosaurs around at the same time?'

No, indeed they weren't. For example, *Stegosaurus* and *Triceratops* could never have come face to face, except, perhaps, in a museum. *Stegosaurus* lived in the Jurassic Period whereas the first *Triceratops* didn't walk the Earth until the late Cretaceous Period. Both species may only have survived for two or three million years within those periods. A wide variety of dinosaurs lived on this planet at different times over the total timespan of 165 million years.

Stegosaurus

Triceratops

4 'Why are dinosaurs called dinosaurs?'

There's nothing experts like more than giving things names, whether it's plants, animals or periods in history or prehistory, as we've already seen. Rather than calling these huge animals, whose remains were suddenly turning up everywhere, 'prehistoric monsters', the British scientist

Richard Owen coined the term 'dinosaur' in 1842. It comes from the Greek word *deinos* which means 'terrible' or 'marvellous' and *sauros* which means 'lizard' ... and 'terrible lizard' is a pretty good description, if you ask me. *Iguanodon* was named 17 years before Owen had even come up with the term 'dinosaur', which was to include *Iguanodon* amongst them.

5 'Are dinosaurs just big lizards?'

No, we now know that dinosaurs and lizards are only distantly related. Sir Richard Owen classified them in very particular ways. Dinosaurs had upright legs whereas ordinary prehistoric lizards had sprawled legs (like a typical lizard today). Not only that, dinosaurs had three or more vertebrae (bony segments in the spine) supporting their pelvis, which is another word for the hip bones. In fact, dinosaurs are further divided into two categories, depending on the shape of their hip-bones: saurischia, which are 'lizard-hipped' dinosaurs, and ornithischia, which are 'bird-hipped' dinosaurs. The easy way to remember which is which is that ornithology is the study of birds, so ornithischia must be the bird-hipped ones. (*Ornis* is Greek for 'bird', if you were wondering. Greek and Latin words were – and are still – used a lot for scientific classification.)

THE TWO TYPES OF DINOSAUR

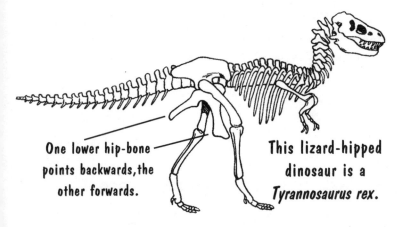

One lower hip-bone points backwards, the other forwards.

This lizard-hipped dinosaur is a *Tyrannosaurus rex*.

The saurischian (lizard-hipped) dinosaurs

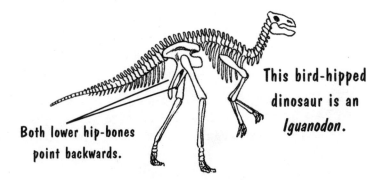

Both lower hip-bones point backwards.

This bird-hipped dinosaur is an *Iguanodon*.

The ornithischian (bird-hipped) dinosaurs

'What's the big deal about dinosaurs?'

The big deal about dinosaurs at the time was that, with their upright legs and supported pelvis, they were better adapted to getting about compared to the other wildlife that was around. (Some scientists believe that their grasping hands and hinged ankle bones played a big part in their success too.) The big deal about dinosaurs in relation to the evolution of the Earth is that they were around for about 165 million years, whilst we true human beings (*Homo sapiens sapiens*) have probably only been around for about 100,000 years. And why are dinosaurs such a big deal to people today? Because they're like make-believe monsters and dragons and aliens that not only really did exist but they actually lived on this self-same planet. And that's a pretty big deal, wouldn't you say?

'Which was the first dinosaur?'

Until recently, we thought his name was Brian and he was an *Eoraptor*. No, I made up the Brian part. We don't know for sure which the very first kind of dinosaur was but, until very recently, the earliest-known dinosaur remains to be found were about 228 million years old. They were discovered in Argentina by a man called Paul Sereno and he called his dinosaur *Eoraptor*, which means 'dawn hunter'... but, in October 1999, the fossilised remains of a 230-million-year-old dinosaur were found in Madagascar, an island off the south-east coast of Africa. Who knows, an even older dinosaur might be discovered tomorrow, or the day after. Maybe even by one of you. One of the first dinosaurs was *Procompsognathus*. It ran around on its hind legs and ate smaller animals, such as big insects and small mammals. One of the first large dinosaurs was *Plateosaurus*. A fully grown one was about 9 metres (29 feet) long. It was a plant-eater. Two of the very earliest dinosaurs were *Herrerasaurus* and *Staurikosaurus*.

'Where was the first dinosaur born?'

No one knows the answer to that, so I don't have an address. What we do know, though, is that the first dinosaurs lived on one huge area of land – a supercontinent – so big that it stretched from the North Pole to the South Pole, surrounded by the Earth's one enormous ocean. This was in the Triassic Period, 220 million years ago. The supercontinent (called Pangaea) and the ocean (the Panthalassa Ocean) aren't there any more. At least, they're not the same shape. Over the past 220 million years, the land has moved to form new continents, islands and oceans to create the familiar globe we now know. And it's worth remembering that the Earth's land masses are still on the move today, but very slowly!

THE CHANGING EARTH

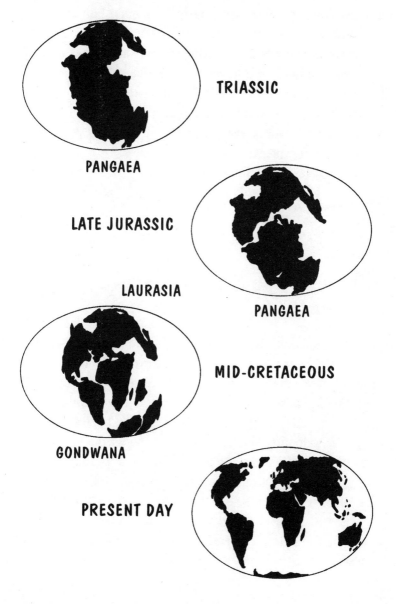

TRIASSIC

PANGAEA

LATE JURASSIC

LAURASIA

PANGAEA

MID-CRETACEOUS

GONDWANA

PRESENT DAY

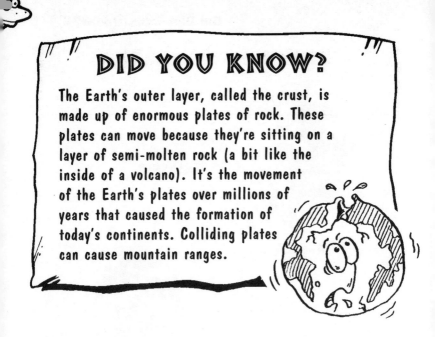

DID YOU KNOW?

The Earth's outer layer, called the crust, is made up of enormous plates of rock. These plates can move because they're sitting on a layer of semi-molten rock (a bit like the inside of a volcano). It's the movement of the Earth's plates over millions of years that caused the formation of today's continents. Colliding plates can cause mountain ranges.

'Were all dinosaurs big and nasty?'

No way, and don't forget that even the dinosaurs you think of as being 'nasty' were just trying to eat, survive and protect their young. They were vicious, yes, but probably not thinking nasty thoughts! During their 165-million-year existence, dinosaurs came in all shapes and sizes. Some hypsilophodontids, for example, were about the size of a sheep and, like sheep, were herbivores (they didn't eat meat). It's true that many remains which have been found are of huge dinosaurs, but that says as much about how remains have survived all this time as it does about the dinosaurs themselves. Have a look at the answer to question 15.

10 'Why didn't all the meat-eating dinosaurs just eat all the non-meat-eating dinosaurs that couldn't bite back?'

What a brilliant question. The answer is that, just because plant-eaters might not have the sharp teeth that the meat-eaters had, it didn't mean that they were defenceless. For example, in the Triassic Period, *Plateosaurus* was not only a plant-eater but also the biggest animal on dry land on Earth, 9 metres long (over 29 feet) and probably weighing over 4 tonnes, no animal in their right mind was going to argue with something that big! And, in later periods, *Plateosaurus* was going to seem tiny compared to some of the new types of plant-eaters that came along... One of the best defences for plant-eating dinosaurs was always their sheer bulk: THEIR SIZE.

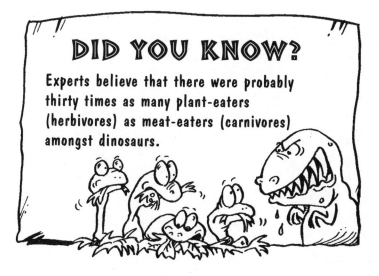

DID YOU KNOW?

Experts believe that there were probably thirty times as many plant-eaters (herbivores) as meat-eaters (carnivores) amongst dinosaurs.

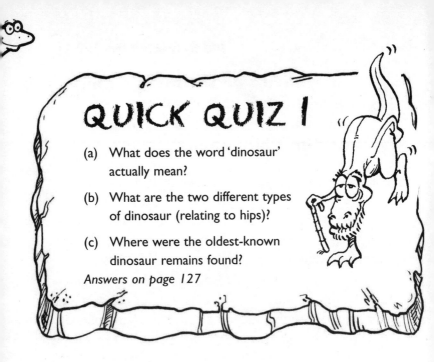

QUICK QUIZ 1

(a) What does the word 'dinosaur' actually mean?

(b) What are the two different types of dinosaur (relating to hips)?

(c) Where were the oldest-known dinosaur remains found?

Answers on page 127

'Is it true some dinosaurs used their tails as weapons?'

It certainly seems that way. A familiar dinosaur is *Stegosaurus*, with its very distinctive armour plates running down its back. (See the illustration on page 14.) In addition to its size and armour plating, though, it also had four huge spikes on its tail, and there's only one logical thing they can have been used for: fighting. *Tuojiangosaurus* had a spiked tail too. *Euoplocephalus*, however, had a swishy tail with a large club on the end, which would have been ideal for hitting its enemies with, giving them an ankle-crushing blow.

'Which was the biggest dinosaur in the world?'

The biggest dinosaurs all come from the same group of dinosaurs called the sauropods (which means 'reptile feet'). Sauropods include *Diplodocus* and *Apatosaurus* which were very big, but even these looked small next to

Brachiosaurus. For a long time, experts thought *Brachiosaurus* was probably the biggest dinosaur there was. A human could have walked between the back legs of a *Brachiosaurus*, under its belly and out through its front legs with plenty of headroom. With its long neck, its head was about 13 metres (43 feet) from the ground! In the 1970s, parts of two even bigger types of dinosaur were found. They've been named *Supersaurus* and *Ultrasauros*. Scientists are hoping to find a whole skeleton of each one day. Now evidence of an even BIGGER dinosaur called *Seismosaurus* has been unearthed! The largest meat-eaters were *Giganotosaurus carolinii* and the terrifying *Tyrannosaurus rex*. *Brachiosaurus* was a staggering 22.5 metres long (74 feet) and is thought to have weighed 77 tonnes. *Ultrasauros* could have weighed up to a mind-blowing 130 tonnes. *Tyrannosaurus rex* was 6 metres (20 feet) tall, 14 metres (46 feet) long and weighing in at around 7 tonnes!

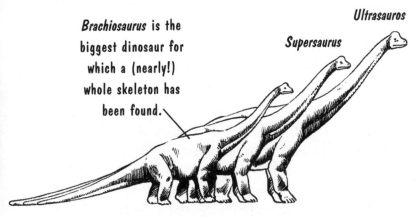

Brachiosaurus is the biggest dinosaur for which a (nearly!) whole skeleton has been found.

Ultrasauros

Supersaurus

Scientists now believe that *Brachiosaurus* and *Ultrasauros* were very alike, and that *Supersaurus* was related to *Diplodocus*.

'If they're only skeletons, how do we know how much they weighed?'

Another brilliant question. The answer is: with a guestimate, which is not quite a guess and not quite an estimate! It's a calculation based on the available facts when there aren't that many around. Of course, there are no dinosaur bodies that can be put on a set of scales and weighed so experts had to find another way. They studied the bone, tissue and muscle weight of similar animals alive today, estimated how much each particular dinosaur might have had, then calculated what the dinosaurs might have weighed from there. Dr Edwin Colbert of the USA is famous for calculating these weights from a series of carefully constructed models.

'Were some dinosaurs really too fat to walk?'

Theories – ideas – are changing all the time. Once it was thought that most dinosaurs were sluggish and slow. Now experts believe that some were very speedy. There were those who believed that the only way that some of the really big dinosaurs could have supported such heavy body weight was by spending most of the time up to their necks in water, with the water supporting their enormous tummies! It's now generally accepted that the amount of water pressure on the dinosaur would have crushed its lungs, stopping it from being able to breathe!

15 'Were most dinosaurs massive?'

Probably not. And this is an important lesson in any branch of palaeontology. Just because most of the dinosaur skeletons that have been found are of big animals, doesn't mean that there weren't plenty of smaller dinosaurs whose skeletons have never been found. It's rare enough for a skeleton to get fossilised and the bones of big dinosaurs had a far better chance of surviving long enough to be fossilised than those of small ones. The bodies of small dinosaurs were far more likely to have been eaten and crunched up, for example, or crushed by rocks.

In other words, there were probably far more kinds of smaller dinosaur that we just don't know about, simply because none of their remains have been found yet. *Compsognathus* is the smallest known dinosaur. An adult could be as small as 70 centimetres (27 inches)... and most of that was tail! That's about the size of a chicken, but it was still a meat-eater. Such mini-meat-eaters lived off insects, worms, small mammals and lizards. In fact, the very first *Compsognathus* skeleton to be discovered had the skeleton of a lizard where its tummy would have been... The remains of one of its last meals!

16 'Which was the fastest dinosaur on Earth?'

By studying body-shape, it's agreed that the honour of being the speediest of dinosaurs belongs to *Struthiomimus*. It was shaped a bit like an ostrich – which is a really fast runner – with a tail, and ran on two three-toed legs. Like an ostrich, it had a beak and no teeth and, like an ostrich, it probably ran up to 50 km/h (31 mph) with good, long strides... as fast as a horse. Experts believe that it ate mainly vegetation and small mammals (and maybe even the odd egg or two). The best use for its speed was probably to escape from all those meat-eaters around towards the end of the Age of the Dinosaurs.

Struthiomimus

Much earlier than *Struthiomimus* – about 125 million years ago, in fact – there lived *Hypsilophodon*. At first, experts believed that its body-shape suggested that it was a tree-climber. Closer study suggested that it too was built for speed. (The bones in its long toes suspected of being used to grasp branches were found not to curl that way.) Its slender body and long legs meant running away was its only real defence!

'What do you call people whose job it is to study dinosaurs?'

Lucky. That was a joke. Get it? 'What do you call...' Oh, never mind. Most dinosaur experts today are called palaeontologists because palaeontology is the study of fossils and that's the state that dinosaur remains are found in. The letters 'palaeo' at the beginning of a word mean 'old', 'ancient' or 'prehistoric'. They come from the Greek *palaios*, meaning 'old'.

'What exactly is a fossil?'

This is an important question because just about EVERYTHING we know about dinosaurs comes from fossilised evidence... and very few of the dinosaurs who were around during those 165 million years have left any fossilised clues. For an animal – or part of it – to turn into a fossil, the conditions have to be just right. Firstly, our dinosaur has to die near water. Then, with luck, its body might end up in it, resting on the bed of the river or lake. The flesh, guts and all the soft bits then rot away or get eaten by other animals, but the teeth, bones and claws – in other words the *hard* parts – remain. Eventually, the skeleton sinks into the bed and is buried in the mud and sand. Over time, the mud turns to solid rock, and the natural chemicals leaking from the rock slowly cause a chemical reaction in the dinosaur skeleton, turning the bones into minerals too. The resulting 'stone' skeletons, claws and teeth are called fossils.

Not all fossils are bones, though. In some cases – including on the beach in the town where I live – fossilised dinosaur footprints have been found. The squishy mud that the dinosaur walked in millions of years ago has turned to solid rock, preserving a record of a single dinosaur's few prehistoric steps.

The reason why these fossils are now found near the Earth's surface – rather than being covered by millions of years of build-up of rock and mud – is because of movements inside the Earth's crust.

DID YOU KNOW?

The word 'fossil' comes from the Latin *fossilis* which simply means 'dug up'!

19 'What can a bunch of old dinosaur footprints tell us?'

Apart from the fact that dinosaurs didn't wear shoes? Quite a lot actually... It's not only amazing to think that a moment in prehistory has almost magically been preserved over millions of years, more accurately than a photograph ever could, but – to the trained expert eye – it can tell us a great deal.

For a start, a particular type of dinosaur can be identified by its footprint and, where there are lots of different footprints, we can tell which dinosaurs are travelling alone and which are in groups. There are hundreds of dinosaur footprints in a place called Lark Quarry in Australia. Here, palaeontologists have pieced together the story of small meat-eating and plant-eating dinosaurs drinking from a waterhole, or eating the vegetation around the edges, when a much bigger meat-eater appeared and they all ran away! It's a bit like detectives re-creating what happened from evidence left at the scene of a crime.

These are *Tyrannosaurus rex* tracks. In real life, the prints would be 6 metres (20 feet) apart.

In a far simpler way, footprints also help us learn the length of a dinosaur's stride and, along with the estimated size and body weight, can be used to estimate how fast they might have been able to run. It is footprints in Broome, Australia, which suggest that there might have been dinosaurs even bigger than *Ultrasauros*.

20 'If all that's left of dinosaurs is old bones, how do we know what colours their skin was?'

The honest answer is that we *don't* know. We can only guess, but it needn't be a wild guess. We know that animal colouring serves four main functions: camouflage, warning, deflecting or attracting heat, and attracting a mate. If you're an enormous *Tyrannosaurus rex*, camouflage is probably not going to be of much use because your supper-to-be is going to see and hear you coming, however much your skin colour blends with the background. If you're a small dinosaur, camouflage will be more useful because it might help you to hide or, if you're small and brightly coloured, it might send out the message 'I may be small, but I'm dangerous. Stay away.' (A bit like a bee or wasp does with its bright stripes.)

There's no reason to believe that all dinosaurs were a boring greeny brown to blend in with their background. Some palaeontologists now believe that some dinosaurs were probably very brightly coloured indeed. We know that they had scaly skin, by the way, because not only have fossilised imprints of dinosaur skin been found (where a dinosaur was lying in mud, for example, and left an impression of its scales) but because some dinosaur fossils have been found with skin still on them. This is extremely rare and has happened in cases where, rather than rotting away, the skin must have dried out and naturally mummified!

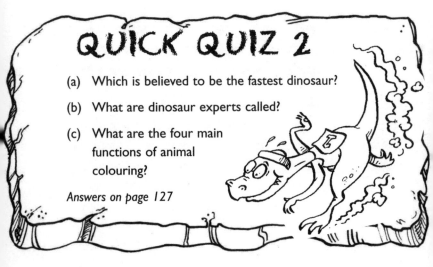

QUICK QUIZ 2

(a) Which is believed to be the fastest dinosaur?

(b) What are dinosaur experts called?

(c) What are the four main functions of animal colouring?

Answers on page 127

2 | 'Do so-called dinosaur experts ever make mistakes?'

O, ye of little faith. Of course they do... see the answer to Question 48, for example. They're only human, and dealing with remains of animals that were around hundreds of millions of years ago. One of the more famous early 'mistakes' was thinking that the thumb spike of *Iguanodon* went on its nose! They also thought it ran around on all-fours. Then they decided that it must have walked upright, its tail trailing behind. Now they think it sometimes walked on two and sometimes four legs, with head low and tail high. Talking of tails, museums – including the Natural History Museum in London – have often displayed *Diplodocus* skeletons with their tails trailing along the ground behind them. Now experts believe that the *Diplodocus* held its tail up, to balance its long neck. The Natural History Museum has now updated its display.

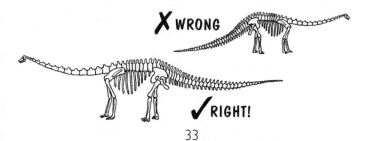

X WRONG

✓ RIGHT!

22 'Did dinosaurs really roar?'

Probably. One of the way scientists can learn about dinosaurs is by studying animals that are still around today, checking for similarities. It seems likely that the terrifying sharp-toothed *Tyrannosaurus rex* roared, and very loudly too. Crocodiles (which are closely related to dinosaurs) can make enough noise to be heard from a very long way off.

Then there's *Parasaurolophus* with its extraordinarily shaped head crest. After much research and testing, modern day palaeontologist David Weishampel believes that they made honking sounds – the bigger the crest, the deeper the sound!

As for a herd of *Parasaurolophus*, the general consensus is that it'd be very noisy indeed! Adult *Parasaurolophus* had long bony crests running from their noses, up between their eyes and over their heads, with the male's crest quite a bit bigger than the female's. Blowing through their crests, they probably sounded like an orchestra of untuned trumpets, each with their own individual noises! Imagine hundreds – thousands even – trumpeting away during the mating season, or if under attack. Argh!!!

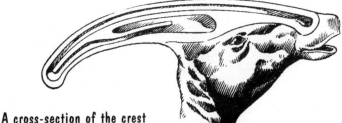

A cross-section of the crest
of a male *Parasaurolophus*.

23 'Did dinosaurs snore?'

This is a GREAT question! It really had me laughing. The things you people want to know! (Or are you just trying to catch me out?) In fact, I like it so much, that's what I'm going to call this book! Well, did they snore? The answer is: probably. Most animals which breathe can breathe heavily, and in their sleep breathe most heavily of all. I imagine that some of the bigger dinosaurs could have been very loud snorers indeed. As for *Parasaurolophus*, imagine what a noise one of them might have made snoring!

24 'Were there the same types of dinosaurs all over the world?'

To begin with, yes, because 'the world' – the Earth – was only made up of one supercontinent, Pangaea from North Pole to South Pole and the climate wasn't that varied – the Poles weren't ice-caps back then, for example. Have a look at the diagram back on page 19. During the early Cretaceous Period (about 127 million years ago) the Pangaea continent had split in two to become two new land masses, including fractured islands. These land masses are referred to as Laurasia and Gondwana, and particular types of dinosaur started to develop in particular areas, unique to that area. (Of course, none of these continents had names at the time, because people weren't around to name them until long after the landscape had changed again.) On the opposite page is a map showing where the remains of certain dinosaurs have been found.

⚄⚄ 'What happened to all the dinosaur poo?'

Some of it still exists as coprolites, or fossilised poo. (Some people prefer to call animal poo 'dung', by the way!) Coprolites from both meat-eaters and plant-eaters have survived. How do we know which is which? Because some contain fossilised seeds, plant stems and even pine cones, whilst others contain bones! Most dinosaur dung will have rotted away millions of years ago, though – in the same way that horse manure and cow pats simply break down over time.

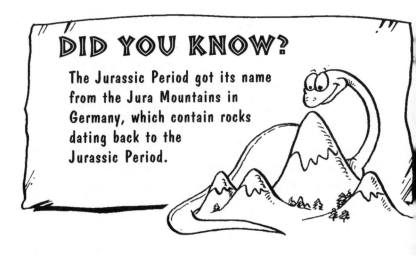

DID YOU KNOW?

The Jurassic Period got its name from the Jura Mountains in Germany, which contain rocks dating back to the Jurassic Period.

WHERE IN THE WORLD?

EUROPE is where the first dinosaur fossils were collected and recorded, in the early 19th century.

European dinosaurs also include: *Platyosaurus, Megalosaurus, Baryonyx* and *Hypsilophodon.*

ASIAN dinosaurs include *Tuojiangosaurus, Velociraptor, Oviraptor* and *Protoceratops.* The Gobi Desert has given up a number of important finds.

AUSTRALIA has had its share of fossil finds, including: *Muttaburrasaurus, Austrosaurus, Leaellynasaura* and *Minmi.*

Iguanodon bones were frequently found on the Isle of Wight.

AFRICA is rich in dinosaur finds, including: remains of *Barosaurus, Brachiosaurus, Spinosaurus* and *Massospondylus.*

NORTH AMERICA is rich with a wide variety of dinosaurs, including: *Triceratops, Stegosaurus, Parasaurolophus, Allosaurus* and the only remains of *Tyrannosaurus rex.* It boasts the Dinosaur National Monument where many key discoveries were made in the late 19th century.

SOUTH AMERICA contains the fossilised remains of the largest meat-eater ever found: *Giganotosaurus.*

26 'Didn't some dinosaurs have beaks?'

Yes, including *Stegosaurus*. A beak was a really useful way for plant-eaters to eat the toughest and chewiest of trees and shrubs. It could act like a really good pair of garden secateurs (scissors) and cut through the thickest foliage. Other dinosaurs had 'snipping' or 'raking' teeth but couldn't chew, which is where gastroliths come in.

27 'Who or what were gastroliths?'

Stones deliberately swallowed by some dinosaurs, especially sauropods. These stones did the job in the stomach that teeth do in mouths: broke up the food to help with digestion. They weren't special stones. Any stone used for that purpose gets labelled a gastrolith. Not all plant-eaters ate stones. Some species had over 900 teeth and could chew perfectly well, thank you very much.

28 'Why aren't flying dinosaurs called dinosaurs?'

Because they weren't dinosaurs, and I can't emphasise that enough: they weren't, weren't, **WEREN'T**! Dinosaurs couldn't fly. The creatures you're thinking of are pterosaurs – winged reptiles – from 'ptero' meaning 'wing'. In the same way there were a variety of dinosaurs, there were a variety of pterosaurs too, though probably not such a wide variety. These included *Pteranodon*, *Eudimorphodon* and *Rhamphorhynchus*. They didn't have feathers. Their wings were stretched skin. As well as clawed feet, they also had claws midway up their wings. In fact, the tip of their wings were really an extra-long fourth finger! In 1970, a pterosaur was found with fossilised fur, like a bat's, which means it was warm-blooded.

PTEROSAURS, <u>NOT</u> DINOSAURS

Eudimorphodon was a long-tailed pterosaur

Claws

Pteranodon had no tail, but a very distinctively shaped head.

These pterosaurs had toothless beaks.

The first pterosaurs appeared **220 million years ago**. That's **10 million years AFTER** the first dinosaurs.

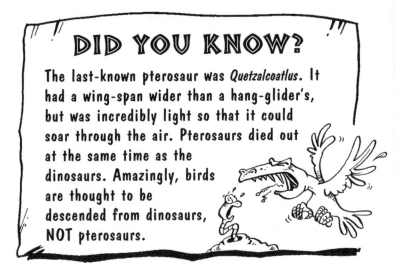

DID YOU KNOW?

The last-known pterosaur was *Quetzalcoatlus*. It had a wing-span wider than a hang-glider's, but was incredibly light so that it could soar through the air. Pterosaurs died out at the same time as the dinosaurs. Amazingly, birds are thought to be descended from dinosaurs, NOT pterosaurs.

 ### 29 'What other kinds of animal were around at the same time as dinosaurs?'

As well as the pterosaurs in the air, there were the ichthyosaurs and plesiosaurs in the sea. (A lot of people imagine that ichthyosaurs and plesiosaurs are the names of underwater dinosaurs. They're not.) These are the names of two different groups of animals altogether. Ichthyosaurs were fish-shaped and plesiosaurs have been described as being 'barrel-shaped'. There were also insects – including dragonflies and cockroaches – small mammals, turtles, crocodiles, and (by the Cretaceous Period) a wide variety of snakes and lizards. None of these mammals would have been bigger than a cat and many were a lot smaller. One such mammal, *Crusafontia* looked a bit like a squirrel with a long nose and probably made rather a nice bite-size snack for a *Tyrannosaurus rex*.

30 'How many kinds of dinosaur are there?'

The remains of about 800 different types of dinosaur have been found, but it's reckoned that there were probably anything up to 3,000 different types, which means that there are still plenty of new ones just waiting to be discovered... which is part of the excitement of palaeontology. No one knows what the next fossil is going to reveal. On average, seven new types of dinosaur are discovered every year.

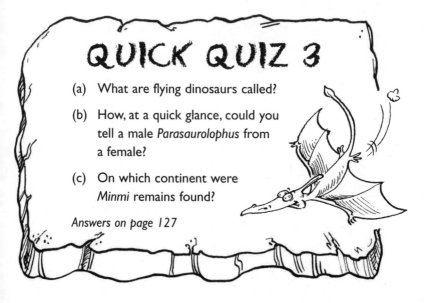

QUICK QUIZ 3

(a) What are flying dinosaurs called?

(b) How, at a quick glance, could you tell a male *Parasaurolophus* from a female?

(c) On which continent were *Minmi* remains found?

Answers on page 127

31 'How long did a typical dinosaur live for?

Hmmm. Why do I suspect that I was asked this question in the hope that I might be stumped! The truth be told, of course, is that – without the aid of a time machine – no one can answer this question with any great confidence. Having said that, it's been worked out that, if the biggest dinosaurs grew at the same rate that elephants grow today, they'd have taken 100 years to fully grow. If you think that's a long time, then hear this: if they grew at the rate that their close relative the crocodile grows today, then the biggest dinosaurs would have to have lived for over 300 years, which is a ripe old age by human standards!

32 'Did dinosaurs really lay eggs?'

Oh yes indeed. The first fossilised dinosaur eggs to be discovered were found in 1859 in France. Whole nests of them were then uncovered in the 1920s in Mongolia. Different dinosaurs arranged their eggs in different ways. Some left them in a higgledy-piggledy state whilst others left them in a carefully-arranged arc or lined up neatly in pairs. Dinosaur nests were rather like craters, probably sometimes filled with leaves. The size of the nest depended on the size and number of eggs.

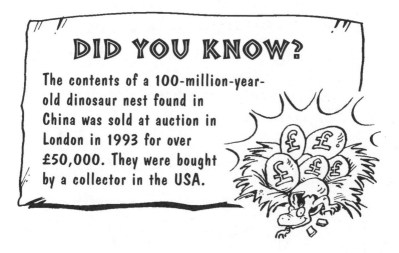

DID YOU KNOW?

The contents of a 100-million-year-old dinosaur nest found in China was sold at auction in London in 1993 for over £50,000. They were bought by a collector in the USA.

33 'Were dinosaurs good parents?'

Most snakes and lizards today simply lay their eggs, usually bury them, and leave their little ones to fend for themselves when they hatch. (Think of those TV documentaries showing tiny turtles having to make it from their sandy nests down the beach to the sea, without a mum or dad turtle in sight.) Palaeontologists used to think that dinosaurs probably behaved in the same way. Then a discovery made in 1978 changed all that. It was a nest full of *Maiasaura* eggs and young, and the experts used all their detective skills to note that:

 the eggs had been carefully positioned — narrow end down — so they wouldn't fall over.

 the little hatched dinosaurs had worn-down teeth which meant that they had been eating whilst they were still in the nest, so someone must have been feeding them. Their parents must have brought them food.

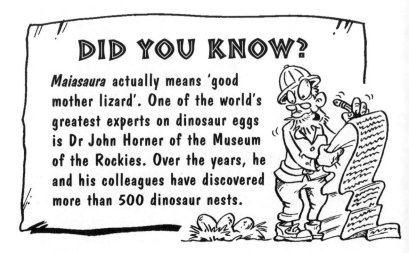

DID YOU KNOW?

Maiasaura actually means 'good mother lizard'. One of the world's greatest experts on dinosaur eggs is Dr John Horner of the Museum of the Rockies. Over the years, he and his colleagues have discovered more than 500 dinosaur nests.

'When were the first dinosaur remains discovered and who by?'

People have probably been discovering fossilised remains of dinosaurs for thousands of years without, of course, having the foggiest idea what they were. Thousands of years ago, 'dragon bones' were discovered in China and it's more than likely that they were actually fossilised dinosaur remains. It was in the 19th century that the real interest in dinosaurs was born and the first major discoveries were made. Gideon Mantell, a Sussex doctor, found the remains of teeth of an enormous, unknown animal in 1820 which, in 1825, he called *Iguanodon* (because the teeth reminded him of those of a giant Iguana lizard). Dean William Buckland of Oxford University studied dinosaur remains found in 1816, and named the creature they belonged to *Megalosaurus*, in 1824.

Both these animals were named before the actual term 'dinosaur' was created by Sir Richard Owen of the Natural History Museum, London. Though he studied fossil finds made by other people around Europe, it was he who realised that they were remains of some distinct group of long-died-out giant reptiles and gave them the name.

One of the greatest early collectors of dinosaur remains in the USA, if not the world, was John Bell Hatcher. In 1888, he was the first person to discover the remains of a *Triceratops*: its skull with very impressive horns. No one knew that any dinosaurs had horns until then.

Triceratops

Triceratops comes from a group of dinosaurs called the ceratopians, which means 'horned face'.

The world's largest mounted dinosaur skeleton (put together and mounted in its original form in a museum) was *Brachiosaurus*, the first bones of which were discovered in 1907 by the German Eberhard Fraas.

Today, there are plenty of palaeontologists still making exciting finds, but it's not just the professionals who make them. Some people have made discoveries quite by chance, and amateurs, such as Englishman Bill Walker, have helped play an important part in widening our knowledge about dinosaurs. In 1982, he discovered the claw of an unknown dinosaur now named *Baryonyx walkeri* after him! Two of the most famous 19th-century American dinosaur 'hunters' were so eager to out-do each other that they became involved in 'Bone Wars'!

'What were the dinosaur Bone Wars?'

In the 1870s and 1880s two men, Othniel Charles Marsh and Edward Drinker Cope, competed to become the top dinosaur fossil collector of the USA! They both hired armed men to protect them against any unfriendly Native Americans they might run into, and against each other. There were a number of well-reported occasions when Marsh and Cope's men were involved in punch-ups! These crazy antics soon earned the nickname the 'Bone Wars'. Amazingly, the two rivals had originally been friends and gone on many of their early dinosaur field-trips together. Despite this ridiculous rivalry-gone-too-far, Marsh and Cope ended up discovering 136 new types of dinosaur between them!

 'Might there be a whole dinosaur preserved in a block of ice somewhere?'

Aha! I suspect this question was inspired by those occasional discoveries of woolly mammoths in glaciers. The important thing to remember here is that dinosaurs had died out long, long, l-o-n-g before the most recent Ice Age iced up the planet, so it's on the extremely side of unlikely that anyone's ever going to find one perfectly preserved in ice... Some dinosaurs may originally have been frozen in ice but, with the climate changes which followed, would have heated up, thawed out and rotted away in the dim, distant past.

DID YOU KNOW?

In France in 1856 workmen digging a tunnel found a pterodactyl – a prehistoric flying lizard, not a dinosaur – in a rock. They claimed it flapped its wings, gave a croak and then died... which is mighty impressive considering it had been fossilised for millions of years!

 37 ### 'Can DNA really be used to bring dinosaurs back to life?'

B-B-ehind you! Actually, not yet. We're back in the *Jurassic Park* territory of Question 2, where (in the book and film) dinosaurs are re-created using dinosaur DNA found inside a mosquito that had fed off dinosaur blood millions of years ago and then, itself, been preserved in amber. Amber is tree sap which was soft and sticky but, over millions of years, has become solid.

Biting insects from the time of the dinosaurs really have been preserved in amber but we're a long way off from extracting their own DNA (the building blocks of life), let alone any from a dinosaur they might have bitten.

'If dinosaurs had such tough skins, how come mosquitoes could bite them?'

It's true that most dinosaurs – even those without the real armour plating of other species – will have had pretty tough skin, but insects could have concentrated on the soft skin areas such as around the nose, ears and nostrils to bite and suck the blood from.

 ## 'Dinosaurs were cold-blooded, like lizards, not warm-blooded, like us, weren't they?'

The answer to this takes us all the way back to the reminder at the beginning that, although dinosaur means 'terrible lizard', dinosaurs weren't actually lizards. The truth is, *we just don't know*. It could even be that some dinosaurs were cold-blooded and some warm-blooded.

Cold-blooded animals move slowly and slow down even more when they're cold (at night or in winter, for example), but experts believe some dinosaurs moved good 'n' fast, which suggests that they might have been warm-blooded...

...but warm-blooded animals have to eat more food than cold-blooded in order to generate that warmth, so the largest plant-eating dinosaurs would have had to eat a staggeringly ENORMOUS amount of food if they were warm-blooded... so maybe they were cold-blooded, so we're back where we started.

There are, of course, other clues but none of them is 100% conclusive. Some people believe that the plates on the back of dinosaurs such as *Tuojiangosaurus* were designed to absorb the sun's heat to help keep the dinosaur warm, which suggests it was cold-blooded, but others say that they were warm-blooded and these plates were to cool them down. Others argue that the plates were to do with defence, not temperature control at all!

Spinosaurus had a big sail-like ridge along its back.

Some scientists believe it was warm-blooded. When it needed to cool off, they think it pumped blood up to its 'sail' where it could cool off more quickly.
Other scientists think that it was cold-blooded and the 'sail' was for absorbing the sun's heat!

Then there's the matter of all those dinosaurs with long necks, and there were plenty of those about! Scientists have suggested that these dinosaurs, at the very least, must have been warm-blooded. Why? It has to do with blood pressure. Blood pressure is what keeps the blood flowing around the body. Warm-blooded animals (you, me, but not necessarily the scaly green alien leaning over your shoulder trying to read this) have much higher blood pressure than cold-blooded animals. Some scientists have concluded that long-necked, cold-blooded dinosaurs wouldn't have had high enough blood pressure for the blood to get all the way up those necks to the brain, so they must have been warm-blooded.

It's a good theory, but we just don't know. Like everything else to do with the study of dinosaurs, who knows what new evidence may be discovered? One day, we might be able to answer this question for sure. (PS. Birds, which are the closest living relatives to dinosaurs, are warm-blooded.)

The longest known dinosaur neck belongs to *Mamenchisaurus*, measuring 14 metres (46 feet)

40 'Were dinosaurs stupid?'

'Stupid' is one of those terms that I'm not a big fan of whether it's applied to people or animals. For starters, it's important to remember that there's a difference between intelligence and knowledge. There could be two people of equal intelligence, one of whom is very knowledgeable having had a brilliant education, and the other of whom has very little knowledge because she lives on her own and has never been educated. Everything the second person knows is from what she's discovered herself. That doesn't make her any less intelligent.

We humans can look at animals and feel vastly superior with our understanding of everything from the atom to electricity... but it was very few humans who actually came up with these discoveries and inventions that now benefit us all. There's nothing clever about switching on a TV. You didn't invent the thing!

Dinosaurs survived on their instincts: their instinct to eat, their instinct to have baby dinosaurs, their instinct to protect their young, their instinct to attack or avoid enemies. They probably didn't need to do a great deal more thinking than that.

The size of an average (known) dinosaur's brain in proportion to the size of its body was very small, but these were big, big animals and, anyway, brain size isn't always a sign of intelligence. It's fair to say, though, that it's unlikely they were as intelligent as modern-day mammals such as rats.

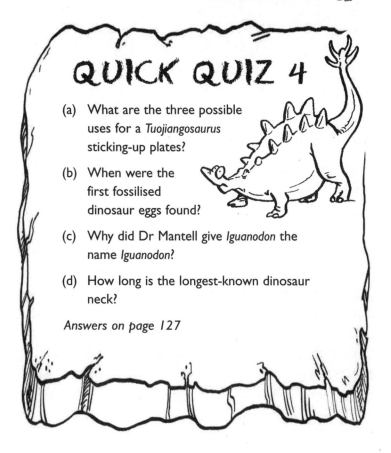

QUICK QUIZ 4

(a) What are the three possible uses for a *Tuojiangosaurus* sticking-up plates?

(b) When were the first fossilised dinosaur eggs found?

(c) Why did Dr Mantell give *Iguanodon* the name *Iguanodon*?

(d) How long is the longest-known dinosaur neck?

Answers on page 127

41 'Which dinosaur had the smallest brain?'

The dinosaur with the smallest brain in proportion to its size was *Stegosaurus*. (You can see how small its head is in relation to the size of its body, back on page 14.) The dinosaur with the largest brain in proportion to its size was *Troodon*. *Troodon* was a small, speedy dinosaur and – although, as I've said before in so many words, a big brain doesn't always equal brainy – experts suspect that *Troodon* was rather smart.

42 'Why did dinosaurs fail and humans succeed?'

Wait a minute! Wait a minute! Is the suggestion here that the dinosaurs died out because they were stupid and somehow 'failed' and then us humans came along and proved ourselves to be far superior? Well, there's only one printable word for that idea and that's: rubbish!

Let's look at the facts one at a time. Firstly, dinosaurs were around for 165 million years. Humans (*Homo sapiens sapiens*) have only been around for about 100,000 years... so we'd better wait another 164,900,000 years before we start judging which of us species was more successful over the same length of time! Then there's the suggestion in the question that dinosaurs died out because they were stupid! In fact, the last dinosaurs probably died out as a result of a single natural catastrophe (see the answer to questions 98 and 99) not because they'd somehow 'failed' to adapt. And then we humans didn't evolve for another 65 million years or so, and here we are waiting to prove ourselves as *successful* as the dinosaurs.

43 'Which was better? Bird-hipped or lizard-hipped dinosaurs?'

If by 'better' you mean which type of dinosaur survived better over millions of years, the answer is neither or both. Both the saurischian (lizard-hipped) and the ornithischian (bird-hipped) dinosaurs evolved over millions of years, but there's nothing to suggest that one group was superior to the other group and would eventually replace the other. Of course, we'll never know for sure because nature intervened and wiped them both out in the end.

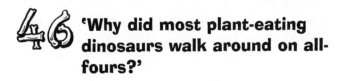

44 'If cavemen and dinosaurs had been around at the same time, could they have tamed one as a pet?'

I love this. It's such a pointless question! Because cavemen – early humans – *weren't* around until millions of years after dinosaurs had breathed their last, it's impossible to answer with any accuracy or meaning. I would suggest that any human – ancient or modern – would be unwise to have anything but the smallest plant-eating dinosaur as a pet... athough, I suspect, even they'd be impossible to house train!

45 'Why were some dinosaurs vegetarians while others ate each other?'

You could ask the same about mammals. Tigers and sheep are both mammals, yet tigers are meat-eaters and sheep are plant-eaters (what you call 'vegetarian'). It's simply how they've evolved and adapted to survive. Over time, animals evolve – change – to adapt to their environment, in order to try to stay alive. (See *A Bit About Evolution* starting on page 117.)

46 'Why did most plant-eating dinosaurs walk around on all-fours?'

You might have thought that it'd have made sense for a

plant-eater to walk around on its hind legs – like a *Tyrannosaurus rex* – in order to reach all those high branches, but the problem was stomach size. A plant-eating dinosaur had to eat an awful lot of food to get the same amount of goodness and energy as the meat-eaters got from a much smaller amount of meat. This meant that the really big plant-eaters needed great big tummies, and weighed a lot more. There was no way they could balance on two legs!

Giant plant-eaters, such as this *Brachiosaurus*, had pillar-like legs, rather like those of elephants today... except, of course, the elephant and its legs are much smaller.

'What did dinosaurs do all day?'

Hunted or searched for food, ate, bred, and tried to survive. Days were shorter. There was a different gravitational pull of the sun and moon. Not only that, for much of the Age of the Dinosaurs, there weren't even seasons. The weather was just the same all the year round.

'My dad has an old book with a picture of a *Brontosaurus* in it, but I can't find the *Brontosaurus* in any of my dinosaur books. Why not?'

Way, way back in 1877, a man called O C Marsh realised that an incomplete collection of huge bones (mostly from the back half of a skeleton) belonged to an unknown dinosaur, which he named *Apatosaurus*. Two years later, he decided that another incomplete assortment of bones (mainly from the front half of a skeleton, this time) belonged to another unknown dinosaur which he named *Brontosaurus*. The only trouble was, when a more complete skeleton was unearthed in the 1970s, it was discovered that *Apatosaurus* and *Brontosaurus* were two examples of the same dinosaur! Because it had been named *Apatosaurus* before it'd incorrectly been given the name *Brontosaurus*, *Apatosaurus* is the correct term to use. To add to the confusion, the Carnegie Museum in Pittsburgh used to have a skeleton of *Apatosaurus* with a head of *Camarasaurus*, and the whole thing labelled *Brontosaurus*... but not any more!

49 'If dinosaurs were everywhere, why don't we find more dinosaur fossils?'

Another way of looking at it is asking why we've found so *many* dinosaur fossils. The way fossils are formed – as explained in the answer to Question 18 – and the fact that the last dinosaurs died so long ago, you might expect them to be so deep underground that no one would ever find them – yet people discover them by accident here, there and everywhere. Why? Because of huge and violent movements in the Earth's crust over millions of years – described in the answer to Question 8 – in which these lower layers (containing the exciting dinosaur bits) have folded up and over to the surface.

50 'Which is the most common dinosaur?'

If by that you mean which is the type of dinosaur whose remains are most commonly found, the answer is probably duck-billed dinosaurs (hadrosaurs) which lived near the end of the Age of the Dinosaurs. Thousands of remains have been found, sometimes of whole herds of more than 10,000 animals that must have been wiped out in sudden disasters. As I've said before, though, *beware* of what this information might mean. Just because so many hadrosaurs have been found doesn't necessarily mean that there were more of them around than any other type of dinosaurs.

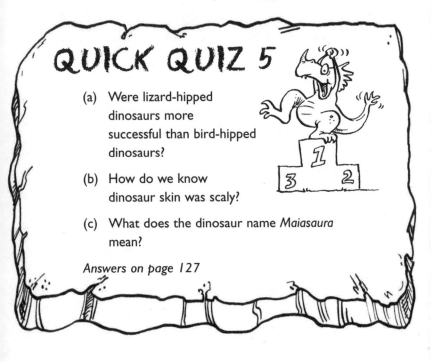

QUICK QUIZ 5

(a) Were lizard-hipped dinosaurs more successful than bird-hipped dinosaurs?

(b) How do we know dinosaur skin was scaly?

(c) What does the dinosaur name *Maiasaura* mean?

Answers on page 127

51 'Which dinosaurs had horns?'

A group of dinosaurs which palaeontologists have called ceratopians, which means 'horned-face'. At first glance, some of the different ceratopians look very similar, but look more closely and you'll see that each had its own distinct horn pattern and neck frill. These frills, at the back of the head, look a bit like the high collars worn by men and women back in Elizabethan England... but, instead of being made of frilly lace, were armour-plated skin and bone. These frills probably acted as a defence (or warning), attracted mates and were the part of the body attached to the animal's massive jaw muscle.

CERATOPIANS
(Horned-faces)

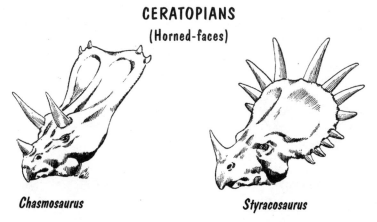

Chasmosaurus　　　　　　　*Styracosaurus*

(Some experts believe that they might also have been brightly coloured.) The horns themselves probably had more than one purpose too. Sure, first and foremost, they were used in defence but they were probably used by males in fights for females (in much the way that stags lock horns today). The size of a male ceratopian's horns might have impressed a possible female mate, showing her what a strong father he would make. This is another example of experts making educated guesses based on studying the behaviour of animals alive today.

Centrosaurus

Torosaurus

Triceratops

Pentaceratops

52 'Did he-dinosaurs look different to she-dinosaurs?'

We know that the bony crest running along the top of the head of a male *Parasaurolophus* was bigger than the crest on a female, as discussed in the answer to Question 22, and some other male dinosaurs probably had bigger horns than the females of the species. Interestingly, one of the biggest differences might have been skin colour. With animals today, there are many examples where the male of the species is far more colourful than the female because he's trying to send out the message "Look at me! Aren't I grand? Choose me as a mate!" The only problem is, as the answer to Question 20 makes clear, we don't actually know what colour any of them were! And that goes for feathered dinosaurs too.

53 'Did some dinosaurs really have feathers?'

Yes, there were, indeed, feathered dinosaurs. Perhaps this is a good time to remind everyone, yet again, that although the term 'dinosaur' means 'terrible' or 'marvellous' 'lizard', dinosaurs weren't lizards, so there's no reason why they should all have been cold-blooded or just had scaly skin. The fossilised remains of *Caudipteryx* were recently discovered in China, showing a faint impression of its feathers. Feathers are an excellent way of keeping warm.

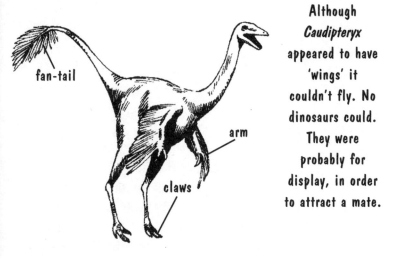

fan-tail

arm

claws

Although *Caudipteryx* appeared to have 'wings' it couldn't fly. No dinosaurs could. They were probably for display, in order to attract a mate.

54 'How did dinosaurs turn into birds?'

It's true that experts believe that birds are the closest descendants of small, meat-eating dinosaurs, but they were a long time coming. The animal which links dinosaurs directly to birds is *Archaeopteryx*. Half dinosaur and half bird, *Archaeopteryx* is often referred to as the 'missing link'... but it can't be missing now, can it, because it's been found?! (The first *Archaeopteryx* fossil was found way back in 1861.) *Archaeopteryx* first appeared at the end of the Jurassic Period. By the end of the Cretaceous Period, however, there were a wide variety of birds, many similar to those we know today... though some of them had teeth!

Archaeopteryx — half bird, half dinosaur — still has claws, but much, much larger wings

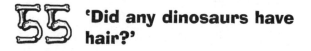

55 'Did any dinosaurs have hair?'

Not in the sense that woolly mammoths had hair or that you and I have hair, or that mammals have fur. They may have had a few wispy bristles, like on the leg of a chicken. At least some of the flying reptiles of the time, pterosaurs (not dinosaurs) were furry, though. See the answer to Question 28.

DID YOU KNOW?

Cockroaches have been around since before the time of the dinosaurs and are still around today. Some sharks have been around even longer.

56 'What were the dinosaurs that lived underwater called?'

Non-existent. There were no such things as underwater dinosaurs. They didn't exist, ever, ever, ever, ever. All right? Ichthyosaurs were fish-eating reptiles swimming around the sea at the same time that dinosaurs were on land and pterosaurs were up in the air. There was another group of fish-eating sea reptiles called plesiosaurs... but neither itchthyosaurs nor plesiosaurs were dinosaurs. They were ichthyosaurs and plesiosaurs, and, like dinosaurs, ichthyosaurs and plesiosaurs came in many different shapes and sizes. The largest ichthyosaur, recently discovered in Canada, was 24 metres (79 feet) long!

57 'Is it true that there was actually a dinosaur with a kind of built-in fish hook?'

Hmmm. I had to think long and hard about this one, trying to work out what the questioner might be thinking of. There were, of course, certain species of pterosaurs – flying reptiles, not dinosaurs – which might have trailed their jaws through the water to catch fish (see the answer to Question 28), but I don't think they'd really count. Then I remembered *Baryonyx*. *Baryonyx* was a dinosaur with one extra-large, hooked claw on each hand, and a long thin mouth with rows of pointy teeth. The hooked claw would have been ideal for spearing fish and the mouth ideal for grasping the fish before swallowing and, guess what, fossilised fish scales have been found in its fossilised tummy... so perhaps *that's* what our questioner was getting at.

58 'What kind of prehistoric monster might the Loch Ness monster be?'

I'm not going to get into the argument as to whether the Loch Ness monster might or might not exist. What I will say, though, is that if I had to choose a prehistoric animal that fitted her general description (from 'eye-witness' accounts), I'd say she was a medium-sized plesiosaur – *not a dinosaur, not a dinosaur, not a dinosaur* – such as a *Muraenosaurus*.

This *Muraenosaurus* is a plesiosaur.

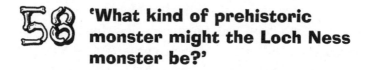

Plesiosaurs and ichthyosaurs ruled the water whilst dinosaurs ruled the land.

'Did dinosaurs smell?'

If you mean were they *smelly*, the answer is that they must have been. All animals smell and some of these were mighty big beasts... and think of all that dinosaur dung! If you mean did they have a good sense of smell, the answer is that it's likely that at least some of them did. The front part of *Iguanadon*'s brain was quite large. This is the part which involves smelling, so it probably used its sense of smell to find food and avoid becoming food. In other words, it sniffed out the juiciest plants whilst keeping a nostril open for the scent of any would-be attackers.

60 'Where are dinosaurs' ears?'

Don't worry, they're there – one on either side of their heads – but, like birds and reptiles, dinosaurs didn't have the sticky-out bit of the ear (which is called the pinna) so you couldn't see them very easily. The hunting dinosaurs, including the likes of *Tyrannosaurus rex*, probably had excellent hearing. There'd also have been little point of *Parasaurolophuses* trumpeting their own individual noises through their crests – see the answer to Question 22 – if they didn't also have good enough hearing to tell these sounds apart.

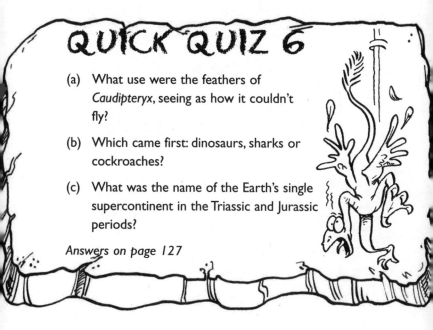

QUICK QUIZ 6

(a) What use were the feathers of *Caudipteryx*, seeing as how it couldn't fly?

(b) Which came first: dinosaurs, sharks or cockroaches?

(c) What was the name of the Earth's single supercontinent in the Triassic and Jurassic periods?

Answers on page 127

Okay, okay, so there's one dinosaur that I get asked more questions about than any other and that — no prizes for guessing — is our old friend *Tyrannosaurus rex*. So, with a break from tradition, the next ten questions are all given over to that one mighty monster.

61 'Why do people say that *Tyrannosaurus rex* is king of the dinosaurs?'

'*Tyrannosaurus rex*' means 'king tyrant lizard'. 'Rex' means 'king'. It probably earned that name from being such a mind-boggling killer dinosaur. It was a huge, upright-walking, lizard-hipped dinosaur over 6 metres (20 feet) tall and 14 metres (46 feet) long... with fifty enormous, razor-sharp teeth and feet equipped with powerful claws.

62 'Was *Tyrannosaurus rex* really as big as a killer whale?

Bigger. TWICE as big, in fact. It may have weighed about the same as a killer whale (8 tonnes), but was double the size and double the trouble!

63 'Is there really a *Tyrannosaurus rex* called Sue?'

Yes. In 1990, the most complete *T rex* skeleton ever was found in South Dakota in the USA. The palaeontologists who found it claimed it was theirs. The local government who owned the land claimed it was theirs, and the farmer who leased the land off them and farmed it claimed it was his. The courts decided in favour of the farmer who sold the dinosaur for over $8 million (that's £5 million). With everyone suing everyone else left, right and centre, what better name to give the dinosaur than 'Sue'? So Sue she is, and can now be seen in the Field Museum in Chicago!

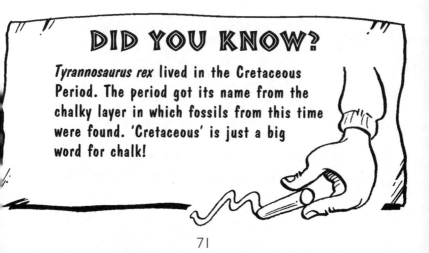

DID YOU KNOW?

Tyrannosaurus rex lived in the Cretaceous Period. The period got its name from the chalky layer in which fossils from this time were found. 'Cretaceous' is just a big word for chalk!

64 'What use were *Tyrannosaurus rex's* tiny front legs?'

Good question. They were certainly far too short to walk on and weren't even long enough for *Tyrannosaurus rex* to hold its food in when feeding – they couldn't even reach its mouth! So, the truth be told, it's really not clear what they were good for. Perhaps the fact that they were so tiny was a vital part of the creature's balance, with the tail lifted off the ground and the back legs in the centre of the body when charging at prey. It might also have needed to use its front legs (or 'arms') to help push itself up from a crouching position. Its meat-slicing teeth, however, were enough of a weapon without needing long arms too!

TYRANNOSAURUS REX

There are very few fossil remains of this vicious meat-eater and only twelve or so of these are fairly complete skeletons.

65 'Could *Tyrannosaurus rex* crush you like an elephant?'

Yes and no. It was much, much bigger and heavier than an elephant so, if you or any other humans had been around at the time of dinosaurs – which, of course, they weren't – and a *Tyrannosaurus* chose to sit on you, you'd be crushed. Unlike the big plant-eaters (see the answer to Question 46), a *Tyrannosaurus rex*'s legs were nothing like an elephant's. An elephant's legs are pillar-like and it walks on flat foot pads. *Tyrannosaurus rex*'s legs were more like an ostrich's, and it walked on its tip toes. Elephants plod. *T rex*es ran! It also used its powerful, clawed feet to hold down its victims... before slicing into their flesh with those huge teeth.

66 'How fast could *Tyrannosaurus rex* run?'

Like experts in every subject, dinosaur experts can't agree on everything – it would be so much more boring if they did – but there are two main schools of opinion on speeding *Tyrannosaurus*. Most believe they could have reached a perfectly respectable top speed of 25 km/h (15 mph) whilst one has calculated that it could probably run as fast as a rhino: 65 km/h (40 mph). It would have lifted its tail off the ground and swayed it side-to-side to counterbalance its massive body on the move. The fastest of us humans can run at about 36.5 km/h, (22.7 mph).

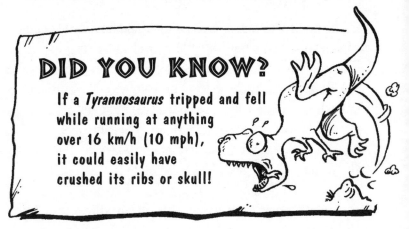

DID YOU KNOW?

If a *Tyrannosaurus* tripped and fell while running at anything over 16 km/h (10 mph), it could easily have crushed its ribs or skull!

67 'Is it true that *Tyrannosaurus rex* had such bad eyesight it hunted by smell?'

No way! It probably had a good sense of smell and hearing, like any good hunter, but *Tyrannosaurus rex* had excellent eyesight too. Many dinosaurs had their eyes on the sides of the head, which was an excellent way of seeing what was going on in the general area all around them, but not so good for getting a clear picture of what was up ahead. Like humans, however, *T rex* is thought to have had its eyes on the front of its head, so could keep its eye clearly on its next victim: lunch.

Eyes-front view   Eyes-at-the-side view

68 'Why is *Tyrannosaurus rex* the most famous dinosaur of all?'

Not for any scientific reason but probably because it's the most exciting and most frightening. Of all the prehistoric monsters of land, sea or air, *Tyrannosaurus rex* is the most terrifying and truly monster-like that we know of. It didn't just plod about eating leaves but was on the prowl with glinting teeth and claws... and it's not some make-believe creature, either. It really walked the Earth and has somehow managed to capture people's imaginations.

69 'Is tyrannosaurid just another name for *Tyrannosaurus rex*?'

No. All *Tyrannosaurus rex* are tyrannosaurids, but not all tyrannosaurids are *Tyrannosaurus rex*! Tyrannosaurids are the family – the group – that a number of similar dinosaurs belong to, including *Tyrannosaurus rex*, *Albertosaurus* and *Tarbosaurus*. Both *Albertosaurus* and *Tarbosaurus* were smaller than *Tyrannosaurus rex*, but were still vicious predators.

70 'Where in the world have *Tyrannosaurus rex* remains been found?'

So far, only in western North America. *Tyrannosaurus rex* lived near the end of the Cretaceous Period and near the end of the Age of the Dinosaurs. By now, the land mass of the Earth had split from the one great continent of the Triassic Period into separate continents, so animals couldn't move so freely as before. (See the maps on page 19.)

DID YOU KNOW?

All dinosaurs have two names, not just *Tyrannosaurus rex*. The first name is the genus and the second the species. Most dinosaurs are only referred to by their genus. Because the *T rex* is everyone's favourite, it often gets special treatment and both names get used!

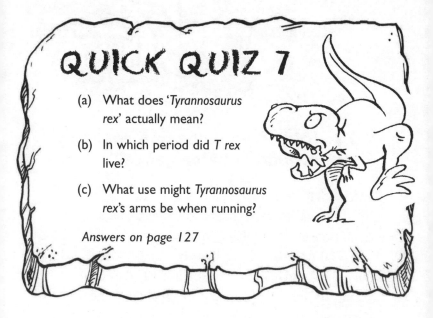

QUICK QUIZ 7

(a) What does 'Tyrannosaurus rex' actually mean?

(b) In which period did T rex live?

(c) What use might Tyrannosaurus rex's arms be when running?

Answers on page 127

77

71 'Did some dinosaurs really go around in killer gangs?'

There's evidence that some meat-eaters (carnivores) hunted in packs. The really big meat-eaters, such as *Tyrannosaurus rex*, probably hunted alone, or in twos and threes, but experts believe that the smaller ones, such as *Velociraptor*, did hunt in groups. That way they could share a meal of an animal much bigger than themselves. *Velociraptor* wasn't much bigger than a goat, but had huge claws and a very long tail... and a whole pack of them could do a lot of damage. They could run fast and bite hard.

DID YOU KNOW?

Dinosaurs were lucky. If their teeth broke or wore away with all that teeth-sinking, flesh-tearing or plant-chewing, they kept on growing new ones — something which doesn't happen with us humans!

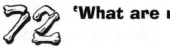

72 'What are raptors?'

A group of dinosaurs which included *Velociraptor* (named after their supposed speed; *velocitas* means swift), and *Utahraptor* (named after Utah in the USA where a *Utahraptor* fossil was found). Both had an out-sized sickle-shaped claw on each foot, ideal for slashing open the flesh of their prey whilst standing on them. Yerch! Thank heavens for pre-packed food at supermarkets.

DROMAEOSAURUS

Yet another raptor: fast-moving, vicious and with those
sickle-like claws

73 'Did some dinosaurs live in herds like zebra and antelope do?'

Even if there wasn't the evidence of remains and footprints that there is, it'd be a pretty safe bet to say that some did, for protection and food. If you're a group of slow-moving plant-eaters without sharp teeth, sharp claws or the means of a speedy getaway, it would make sense to have safety in numbers, with more pairs of eyes on the lookout for danger, and the children protected in the middle. (See the answer to Question 22.)

74 'Were some dinosaurs cowards?'

All animals have a built-in instinct for survival but also different ways of coping with life. In human terms, the modern-day bird, the cuckoo, 'abandons' its young and is 'lazy' because it doesn't even bother to build its own nest. The adult cuckoo is 'bad' because it pushes another bird's eggs out of the nest and then replaces it with a cuckoo egg, leaving the other 'poor old' bird to hatch and feed the baby cuckoo, thinking it's its own offspring.

But is the cuckoo really lazy and bad? Of course not. That's the way that the cuckoo has evolved and it knows no other way of successfully continuing the cuckoo line. It wouldn't know how to build a nest, even if it wanted to!

It must have been the same with dinosaurs. Some evolved

to take more risks than others, so some species might have appeared to be 'more cowardly' than others... but that's a very human way of looking at things!

75 'Why did some harmless dinosaurs have armour and others have none?'

If a lot of what we think of as 'armour plates' actually turn out to have had more to do with temperature control, as discussed in the answer to Question 39, then the answer here might be that it depended on the climate where they lived. It's also down to the fact that different dinosaurs developed in different ways. A really, really HUGE plant-eater may have seemed defenceless without any 'armour', but its huge size was an excellent defence, so it didn't need additional lumps and bumps and spikes and plates.

DID YOU KNOW?

The spikes on the tail of a *Stegosaurus* could grow to be over 1 metre (3 feet) long! The bony club on the end of an *Ankylosaurus*'s tail was strong enough to smash a predator's ankles.

76 'Are crocodiles direct descendants of dinosaurs?'

No, but they had the same ancestors. There was a group of reptiles called the archosaurs and both the dinosaur and the crocodile evolved from them. 'Archosaur' means 'ruling reptiles'. Before the archosaurs, reptiles had sprawling legs, like their amphibian ancestors. The first archosaur to develop legs under the body (rather than at the side like an ordinary lizard) were a group called thecodonts. They could walk almost upright. These strong back legs and tail had developed for swimming, but proved successful on land too. Dinosaurs and crocodiles both evolved from the thecodonts, the most primitive archosaurs.

77 'How long did it take for ordinary reptiles to evolve to dinosaurs?'

Reptiles first appeared on Earth during the Carboniferous Period, round about 310 million years ago. It was about 180 million years later (that's 200 million years ago) that the first true dinosaurs appeared – with a whole string of other creatures in between, forming the links in the evolutionary chain from one type of creature to the other. (See *A Bit About Evolution* on page 117.) Reptiles didn't just evolve into dinosaurs, of course. Some eventually became plesiosaurs, living in the sea (see the answer to

Question 56) and pterosaurs, up in the air (see the answer to Question 28). Some even evolved into mammals. The word 'reptile' comes from the Latin *repere*, meaning 'to crawl'... and with their upright legs and special hips, crawling is something that dinosaurs just don't do! Today, there are about 6,500 different types of reptile on the loose.

78 'Did I imagine it, or did some dinosaurs really head-butt each other?'

An adult asked me this one, worried that he might have been confusing real dinosaurs with something he'd seen in a monster movie. Well, the answer is: no, you didn't imagine it. Near the end of the dinosaurs' time on Earth, a group of dinosaurs called the pachycephalosaurs (which means 'thick-headed lizards') evolved. Some people call them 'boneheads'! They were plant-eaters that stood on their two hind legs and had really, really thick skulls.

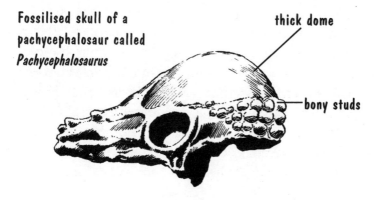

Fossilised skull of a pachycephalosaur called *Pachycephalosaurus*

thick dome

bony studs

This pachycephalosaur is *Stegoceras*.

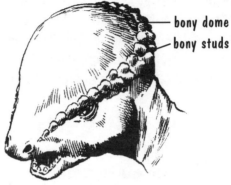

bony dome
bony studs

The biggest of all the pachycephalosaurs was *Pachycephalosaurus*, which was over 4.5 metres (15 feet) tall. The smallest pachycephalosaurs were not much bigger than a chicken – but they all had one thing in common: head-butting. Experts believe that the adult males had head-butting contests to win female mates. (In much the same way that the male ceratopians locked horns in the answer to Question 51.) Their skulls were probably thicker than females.

It wasn't just a pachycephalosaur's extra thick dome on the top of its skull that made it such a remarkable head-butter. The way the neck, backbone and hips evolved ensured that it could thrust its head forward and absorb the shock of such powerful clashes. The brain itself was cushioned beneath the solid bony dome at the top of the head. Without such protection, a single head-butt could have easily caused brain damage or even killed it!

 **'Which dinosaur had the biggest head?'**

The biggest skull of any known land animal belongs to *Torosaurus*. (There's a picture of a *Torosaurus*'s head back on page 62.) A ceratopian (horn-faced) dinosaur, its skull was about 2.4 metres (nearly 8 feet) long!!!

DID YOU KNOW?

The crest on the head of a *Corythosaurus* would have been no good for head-butting or even as defence. It would have snapped off. Experts think, therefore, that it must have been there to look nice: to attract a mate and, maybe, even make sounds (like *Parasaurolophus*).

 'Why didn't any dinosaurs have armour or spikes on their tummies?'

A good point. However well protected a dinosaur was, it had a soft underbelly... relatively speaking of course! (Dinosaur skin would seem pretty tough to us.) Even today few, if any, land animals have protection on their actual bellies. Rhinos have horns and lions teeth but, like dinosaurs, their tummies don't have additional protection. A tortoise may have the protection of its shell and a hedgehog may be able to roll itself up into a spiky ball, but their actual bellies are soft and smooth.

The reason is straightforward enough. Imagine trying to lie on a spiky belly, or to mate or to move about with one. A smooth underbelly ensured comfort and ease of movement. It was the one area that a dinosaur needed all its other armour, weight and 'weapons' to protect. It was every dinosaur's weak spot.

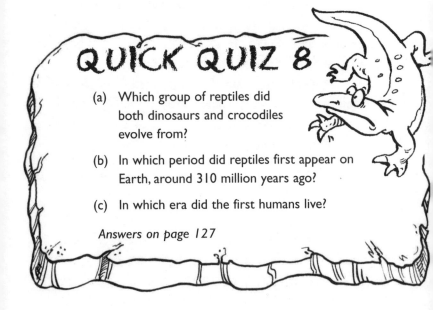

QUICK QUIZ 8

(a) Which group of reptiles did both dinosaurs and crocodiles evolve from?

(b) In which period did reptiles first appear on Earth, around 310 million years ago?

(c) In which era did the first humans live?

Answers on page 127

81 'What sort of plants did plant-eating dinosaurs eat, and were there enough to go round?'

There wasn't any grass during the age of the dinosaurs – a very popular source of food with many herbivores today – and there weren't many flowering plants either. Most of the trees were like the conifers we have today with needles as leaves. There were also plenty of ferns and smaller shrubs with big and what has been described to me as 'waxy' leaves. As already discussed in the answer to Question 46, plant-eaters had to eat a huge amount of vegetation, hence their walking around on all-fours to support their big tummies!

There probably wouldn't always have been enough food to go around, especially when the land masses of the Earth were shifting (as shown on page 19) and the climate was changing. Some dinosaurs would have been cut off from large areas of food supply and some plants would have died as a result of the changes of climate.

Some dinosaurs – such as *Apatosaurus* – moved in big herds, eating all the vegetation in one place and then moving on in search of more food. This was bad luck for the next lot of dinosaurs to arrive after them. The leaves would have been stripped bare.

82 'What did the very little meat-eating dinosaurs eat?'

A good question when you remember that many plant-eaters were safe from attack from them because of their sheer size, and that not all meat-eaters were as big and ferocious as *Tyrannosaurus rex*. The answer is that they ate insects – there were plenty of big and meaty dragonflies about – lizards and the few early mammals that were beginning to establish themselves on the planet. Most of these mammals would have been no bigger than a mouse, so were easy prey.

83 'Did all meat-eaters go around on two feet and all plant-eaters on all-fours?'

As far as we know, all meat-eaters went around on their hind legs, but some plant-eaters went around on all-fours and some upright on two... then, of course, there were omnivores. There's more about them in the next answer.

84 'Did meat-eating dinosaurs have to eat their vegetables too?'

Not really, except for a very small, select group called the omnivores. Herbivores ate plants, carnivores ate meat, and

omnivores ate 'meat and veg' as you might put it: they were both meat- and plant-eaters. These included the rather fast-moving and ferocious *Oviraptor*, so the diet must have suited them!

85 'What's a duck-billed dinosaur?'

Duck-bills, also known as hadrosaurs, had long, flat snouts like ducks' beaks (or bills) – not that there were any ducks around then, of course. The name is a modern comparison. Despite the beak itself having no teeth, the sides of their jaws were lined with sharp, grinding teeth. The name 'hadrosaur' has nothing to do with beaks though, it means 'bulky lizard', though all hadrosaurs were agile enough to walk on two feet. Hadrosaurs came in two main groups: the hadrosaurines (with their flat-topped heads) and the lambeosaurines (with a hollow head crest).

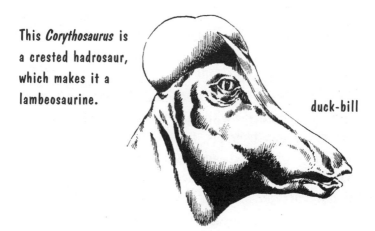

This *Corythosaurus* is a crested hadrosaur, which makes it a lambeosaurine.

duck-bill

86 'Did dinosaurs see in black and white like dogs do?'

As I've mentioned before, the dinosaurs' closest living relatives are birds and crocodiles which, unlike dogs, see in colour. There is, therefore, no reason to suppose that dinosaurs didn't have excellent colour vision. This would help add to the theory that some dinosaurs might have had very colourful, patterned skin to help attract mates. You can find out more about skin colour in my answer to Question 20 and can see how different dinosaurs saw in different ways in the diagram on page 75.

87 'How does a dinosaur fossil get from being in the middle of a rock to being on display in a museum?'

Once a dinosaur fossil has been discovered and its particular position in the layers of rock carefully recorded (as this may help to date it), palaeontologists remove any material covering the top of the fossil. This is very slow, delicate, hard work. The position of each fossilised bone is carefully recorded with photographs and detailed illustrations and diagrams, plotting exactly where every single piece was found and in what position.

Once the top of the dinosaur skeleton has been exposed, they now cut it out of the rock, which can involve anything from chisels to drills, but leave the bones in place. Although the bones have 'turned to stone' they are often very fragile and need to be wrapped in tin foil or even – a popular choice – wet old newspapers. Even once this is done, fossilised dinosaur bones are often additionally wrapped in bandages soaked in plaster of Paris (to form a cast similar to one you'd wear if you broke an arm or a leg) for extra protection on the trip to the museum. Only then are they lifted from the site, put on the truck and driven away.

Each fragment of fossilised bone, however small, is given a code number (written on the cast and recorded) so it can be easily identified once it's at the museum and the skeleton reassembled, like a multi-million-year-old jigsaw puzzle!

Back at the museum, the skeleton is then cleaned, repaired and preserved. The experts who clean and repair fossils go by the name of preparators because they're preparing the fossils for display. Those who coat the fossils with preservatives to harden and protect them are called conservators, because they're conserving – saving – the fossils. Both preparators and conservators are highly skilled technicians.

By this stage, the type of dinosaur will have been identified, and the museum curator will have decided the best way in which the dinosaur skeleton should be displayed to us, the public.

The same dinosaur skeleton can be put in different poses (in much the same way that the original living, breathing dinosaur could move around into different positions). This means that the museums have to decide how they want to display their latest finds: 'running', crouching to 'eat its prey'... the choice is theirs. And this is how a number of mistakes have occurred in the past. (See the answer to Question 21.)

The fossilised bones are treated with a special preservative, wired together and pinned in position at the joints, and then held in position on metal supports. Where dinosaur skeletons on display have very long necks or tails, wires are sometimes suspended from the ceiling and attached to them to give extra support.

What had been trapped in the ground for, at least, 65 million years – and maybe 230 million – is now given a new lease of 'life' for all visitors to see.

'Is it true some dinosaur bones in museums are fakes?'

Fake might not be quite the right word for it! First and foremost, remember that the bones and skeletons you're looking at are fossilised. They've turned to stone. This means that they weigh rather a lot so, in certain instances, a very heavy but fragile skull might be replaced with a plaster of Paris or fibreglass replica of the original, which doesn't weigh so much and won't come crashing down. Also, a complete skeleton always looks more impressive than one with bits missing so, in certain instances, missing bones might be replaced with plaster or, nowadays, fibreglass copies.

Today, in some museums or exhibitions, a number of what we think of as being fossilised dinosaur skeletons are actually very cleverly made fibreglass replicas – but they're clearly labelled as such, so aren't claiming to be something that they're not, which means that they aren't strictly fakes!

There have, of course, been instances where people have tried to trick museums into buying so-called dinosaur remains that aren't what they seem, but that's quite another matter.

89 'How do experts know how old a dinosaur fossil is?'

The oldest way of working out the age of a fossil is stratigraphy. This is quite simply studying the layer of rock the fossil was discovered in. Sedimentary rock layers form over time. They start as soil but are pressurised into becoming rock by the weight of the new layers on top of them. Geologists know the approximate age of each layer so can work out the fossil's age from this.

A more recent method of fossil dating is to do with the fluctuations (changes) in the Earth's magnetic field. As a result, rocks from different times (geological eras) have been affected differently by the different magnetic fields so, themselves, have different magnetic 'signatures'. By testing the rock where the dinosaur fossil was found, its magnetic signature can give a more accurate date than stratigraphy alone.

A third method of fossil dating is radioisotope-dating. You've probably heard of carbon-dating for archaeological finds, but dinosaurs come from such a long time ago that carbon-dating is no good here. Radioisotopes work on a similar principle to carbon-dating but use different elements.

Some elements (found in rocks) are radioactive. They are said to be 'unstable' and decay over time. The good news for scientists is that the decay of a particular element is constant, so they know exactly how long the process takes. By measuring how much a piece of radioactive rock found near the fossil has decayed, they can get an amazingly accurate estimate of the age of the fossil itself.

The fourth method seems really, really obvious once you know it. It's looking for what are called index fossils. Once you've found your dinosaur fossil, you look for other, smaller fossils around it. If one of these is an index fossil – a fossil which earlier research has already shown to have lived for a very specific, limited period of time – then you can really narrow the field of time that your dinosaur lived.

A well-known group of index fossils is the ammonites. Ammonites were very common during the Jurassic and Cretaceous Periods; so common, in fact, that I have a fossilised one in front of me which I'm using as a paperweight. You've probably seen pictures of them in fossil books because of their attractive shape. They were spiral-shelled sea creatures.

A fossilised ammonite

90 'Can I keep a dinosaur skeleton if I find one?'

If you found dinosaur remains on property you actually own – your own back garden – then you could probably get to keep them... but not necessarily if you only rent the property. Either way, if you found a whole fossilised skeleton, you'd need some expert help and advice on freeing, moving and preserving the bones – see the answer to Question 87 – anyway, so you'd probably be better off lending it or donating it to a museum, where they could then find the best way of displaying it with your name as the donor.

If you kept the skeleton, you wouldn't know how to connect the bones and display them, so they'd probably end up in old suitcases and boxes in the loft, as one of those jobs you never quite get around to doing! Ownership of finds can be a complicated business, as you'll see from the answer to Question 63.

QUICK QUIZ 9

(a) What are the four main methods for dating fossils?

(b) What are the experts who clean and repair, rather than preserve, fossils called?

(c) What is an omnivore?

Answers on page 127

91 'Who gets to name dinosaurs?'

Dinosaurs are usually named by the experts who identify them as a new species. Some are named after the dinosaur's physical features, for example '*Microdontosaurus*' means 'tiny-toothed lizard' and '*Pachyrhinosaurus*' means 'thick-nosed lizard'. Some are named after other palaeontologists, such as the *Lambeosaurus*, named after Lawrence Lambe. Others are named after the place where the remains were discovered. This includes the *Denversaurus* named after Denver, Colorado in the USA and the *Albertosaurus* after Alberta in Canada. Some dinosaurs are named after the way experts believe they behaved. For example, '*Velociraptor*' means 'speedy robber'.

92 'Did any dinosaurs use tools?'

This question isn't as daft as it sounds! I don't think a *Tyrannosaurus rex* ever ran around with a set of screwdrivers, but some animals and tools do go together. In the past, one of the big things thought to separate humans from the animals – we're mammals, remember – was that humans used tools and animals didn't. Wrong! If you've ever seen a film of a chimpanzee carefully choosing the right-sized stick then pushing it down the opening of a termite mound to pull out the termites, you'll know that they use tools. Even common garden birds in the UK use particular stones as 'anvils' to smash open snail shells. Having said that, we don't actually have any evidence of dinosaurs being tool-users. Even though certain dinosaurs swallowed stones to help with their digestion – see the answer to Question 27 – this doesn't really qualify as tool use.

93 'Is it true some dinosaurs danced?'

This question, asked by a very young dinosaur fan, resulted in much laughter from her friends around her, so the answer might surprise them. Dinosaurs could well have danced. Some of them, at least. Dances are often a part of the mating ritual between certain animals, particularly certain species of bird. If some dinosaurs, such as *Caudipteryx* had fan-tails and arm feathers – and we know they couldn't fly – they were probably there to attract a mate, and the male dinosaur may well have taken part in a ritual 'dance' to get the female's attention and to show just how handsome he was.

94 'Were the fish in the sea in the time of the dinosaurs the same kind of fish as we have in the sea today?'

Not necessarily the same, but certainly similar. Horseshoe crabs have been around for over 400 million years and relatives of sturgeon for over 200 million, so they'd be as familiar to ichthyosaurs and plesiosaurs as they are to us. The coelacanth – a type of fish which was first common over 300 million years ago – was believed to be extinct until someone caught one off Africa in 1938!

95 'Is the Disney film *Dinosaur* full of mistakes?'

I think that's a bit unfair! The Walt Disney Corporation was out to make entertainment, not a documentary so, sure, it's full of inaccuracies. Dinosaurs certainly couldn't talk, let alone talk English, and some dinosaurs (which had beaks) have been given lips in the film, simply so that their mouths can form the shapes of words as the characters speak. There are also some mammals in the movie that certainly weren't around at the same time as the dinosaurs, and the vegetation has been chosen to look good, not to be prehistorically accurate.

As a dinosaur fan, though, I'd say that anything that gets a whole new generation interested in dinosaurs is a good thing... and then they can find out the discrepancies (changes from the known truth) for themselves.

96 'Which is the question you'd like to have answered which wasn't asked?'

Nothing mind-blowing. One where I could remind people that the ancestors of mammals were actually around *before* dinosaurs, and true mammals for almost as long as them. It's not that mammals started evolving alongside dinosaurs and, through some superiority, survived when dinosaurs didn't. The truth is that dinosaurs had such a grip on the planet that mammals didn't have an opportunity to evolve or multiply that much. The dinosaurs really did dominate life on Earth. It was only once the dinosaurs died out that mammals took over.

97 'If dinosaurs didn't all live in the same period, what killed off the dinosaurs from the earlier periods?'

Excellent question! It's really important to remember that not all dinosaurs were wiped out 65 million years ago and that many had become extinct – died out – for other reasons during the 165 million years that dinosaurs walked the Earth. Animals that adapt to their environment have a better chance of survival and the Cretaceous, Jurassic and Triassic Periods are all *geological* periods. In other words, they're periods that experts can tell apart by the difference in the rock layers – see the answer to Question 89 – which means that there were big geological changes between these periods. To put it another way: with shifts in the Earth's crust (see page 19) and in climate, the environment the dinosaurs were living in changed so dramatically that many couldn't adapt and survive. The few that could adapt, lived on. At least, until the next big change. This is called 'natural selection' and you can read more about it in *A Bit About Evolution* on page 117.

98 'What killed off all the dinosaurs 65 million years ago?'

From being a warm, humid planet the Earth's climate suddenly became much cooler 65 million years ago, and the plant-life changed. Few animals could adapt to such a sudden and dramatic change and the dinosaurs died out.

There had been climate changes before, resulting in more tropical areas and more rain, and by the end of the Age of the Dinosaurs, there were more flowering plants and the Earth began to have different seasons. Sea levels had also changed and new mountain ranges had been formed. So why did this latest change have more effect than earlier changes in the climate? Perhaps because it happened so suddenly.

Many scientists believe that there must have been a specific single event which caused the dinosaurs to die out at once. This is called the 'extinction event' theory and a number of different scientists have a number of different ideas about what it was.

A popular theory was that the shift in the Earth's plates 65 million years ago led to a lot of volcanic activity across the globe, causing fires, huge dust clouds and acid rain blocking out the sun and destroying vegetation.

But there have been many other theories, including everything from changes in the Earth's orbit leading to a drop in the Earth's temperature that furry mammals and feathered birds could survive, but not dinosaurs, to sneaky mammals eating all the dinosaur eggs, or plant-eaters eating all the plants until there were none left. And when the plant-eaters died out, there wasn't enough food for the meat-eaters.

Studies have also been made on the possibility of a sun going supernova (in other words, a star exploding) and showering the Earth with deadly radiation, but that would have been more likely to kill *everything* but the insects.

One of my favourite theories is that these huge plant-eating dinosaurs farted so often and so much that they created a HUGE build-up of methane gas which finally caused the greenhouse effect. resulting in the big changes in the climate!

Today, the most generally accepted 'extinction event' theory is that the Earth was hit by a huge rock from outer space. It's interesting to note, however, that this theory was developed by scientists Luis and Walter Alvarez as recently as 1980 – a little over 20 years ago, at the time I'm answering this question – and, at the time, many experts thought it was a ridiculous suggestion. Now, some people take it to be the undisputed truth. It's important to remember, however, that it's simply the theory that best fits the facts based on current information. For example, iridium, a metal commonly found in meteorites, is rare on Earth and when it is found it's usually in 65-million-year-old rocks.

99 'How could one meteor kill off all the dinosaurs?'

It'd certainly have to have been a VERY big one to squash them all flat at once! The meteor theory suggests that the rock's impact on the Earth not only caused raging fires, volcanic activity, high winds and tidal waves but also a dust cloud and acid rain that blocked out the sun. This would not only have lowered the temperature but would also have killed off the plants (which need sunlight to survive). Those plant-eaters which survived all the other catastrophes would have died of starvation. The remaining meat-eaters would have had to eat each other. Small meat-eating mammals, on the other hand, could live off dead dinosaurs' bodies for quite a while.

100 'Surely such a big meteor would have left a big dent in the Earth?'

Yes, it would indeed have left an enormous 'impact crater', which is simply a more technical term for your equally accurate 'big dent'. In fact, the Earth has been hit by plenty of meteorites over millions of years, but one which is of great interest as far as dinosaurs are concerned is the 193-kilometre-wide (120-mile-wide) crater Chicxulub at the tip of the Yucatán Peninsula in the Gulf of Mexico, Central America. It's over 1.6 kilometres (1 mile) deep. Another crater, from around the same period, is Shiva crater under the Arabian Sea. In pieces now, it's been estimated that this crater would've been 595 kilometres (370 miles) long, 451 kilometres (280 miles) wide and a staggering 12 kilometres (7.5 miles) deep. It's named after the Hindu god of destruction and renewal.

100½ 'Do you know any dinosaur jokes?'

Aha! We finally come to the last question in the book and it's more of a *half* question, really, because it has more to do with jokes than with dinosaurs... Having said that, since I started work on this book, people haven't only been asking me dinosaur questions but have also been supplying me with dinosaur jokes. The only thing is, they're nearly always different versions of the same ones! Do most of these seem familiar?

Q: What kind of dinosaur wears a sombrero?

A: *Tyrannosaurus Mex.*

Q: What kind of dinosaur wears a cowboy hat?

A: *Tyrannosaurus Tex.*

Q: What do you call a short-sighted dinosaur?

A: A *Do-you-think-he-saurus!*

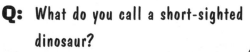

Q: What do you get if you cross gunpowder with a dinosaur?

A: Dino-mite!!!

Q: Which dinosaur kept the other dinosaurs awake?

A: A *Brontosnaurus.*

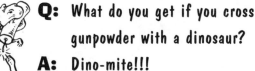

Well, I was bound to include that last joke in a book called *Did Dinosaurs Snore?* now, wasn't I? And it seems a good way to end my answers. Happy dinosaur hunting!

QUICK QUIZ 10

Can you name the following animals?

(a)

(b)

(c)

(They're not to scale)

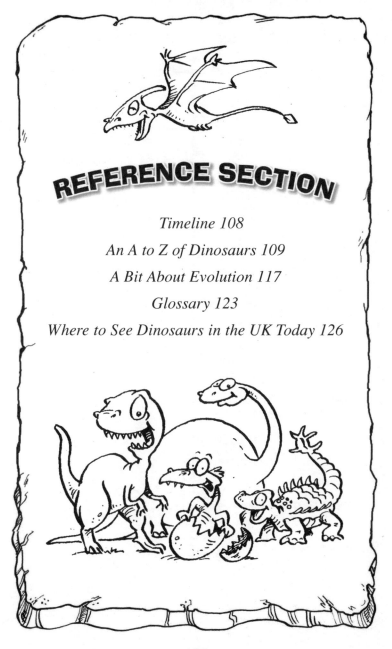

REFERENCE SECTION

TIMELINE

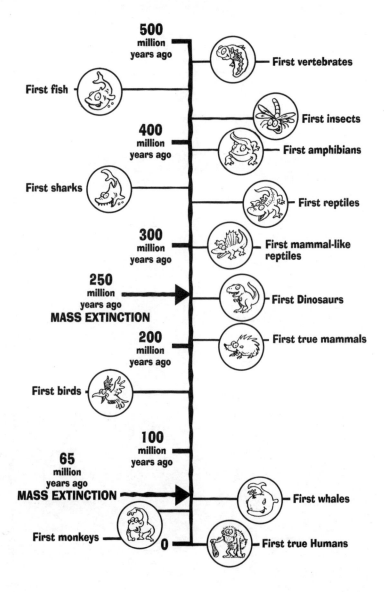

500 million years ago — First vertebrates

First fish

400 million years ago — First insects — First amphibians

First sharks — First reptiles

300 million years ago — First mammal-like reptiles

250 million years ago
MASS EXTINCTION — First Dinosaurs

200 million years ago — First true mammals

First birds

100 million years ago

65 million years ago
MASS EXTINCTION — First whales

First monkeys — 0 — First true Humans

AN A TO Z OF DINOSAURS
What they ate and what they looked like!

 Acanthopholis, spiny, studded plant-eater

Acrocanthosaurus, big meat-eater

Alamosaurus, long-necked plant-eater

Albertosaurus, big meat-eater related to *Tyrannosaurus rex*

Allosaurus, big meat-eater

Amargasaurus, plant-eater with 'sail' along neck, back and tail

Alxasaurus, meat-eater

Anatotitan, large, duck-billed plant-eater

Anchisaurus, plant-eater, walking on both two and four legs

Ankylosaurus, heavily armoured plant-eater with spikes and club tail

Apatosaurus, long-necked, long-tailed plant-eater

B **Bagaceratops,** plant-eater with horned head

Baryonyx, large meat-eater, with 'fish-hook' claw

Brachiosaurus, enormous long-necked plant-eater (stood rather like a giant giraffe)

C **Camarasaurus,** long-tailed plant-eater

Camptosaurus, plant-eater, with longer back legs than front

Carcharodontosaurus, 'sharked-tooth' meat-eater

Carnotaurus, meat-eater with two head horns

Caudipteryx, feathered meat-eater

Ceratosaurus, meat-eater with horn on nose tip

Chasmosaurus, three-horned plant-eater

Coelophysis, meat-eater

Compsognathus, chicken-sized meat-eater. Smallest-known dinosaur

Corythosaurus, large, duck-billed plant-eater with crested head

D **Deinonychus,** meat-eater with sickle-like claws

Dilophosaurus, double-crested meat-eater

Diplodocus, very long-necked, long-tailed plant-eater

Dryosaurus, speedy, horn-beaked, two-legged plant-eater

 Edmontosaurus, duck-billed, ridged-backed plant-eater

Eoraptor, small meat-eater. One of the oldest dinosaurs to be discovered so far

Euoplocephalus, heavily armoured, spiked, studded, club-tailed plant-eater

Fabrosaurus, small plant-eater

Gallimimus, fasting-running omnivore

Giganotosaurus, the biggest of the known meat-eaters

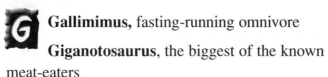 **Hadrosaurus,** duck-billed plant-eater

Herrerasaurus, one of the earliest dinosaurs, a meat-eater

Heterodontosaurus, two-legged plant-eater

Homalocephale, thick-skulled plant-eater

Hylaeosaurus, spiked plant-eater

Hypsilophodon, small plant-eater

 Iguanodon, thumb-spiked plant-eater. The second dinosaur fossil to be named

 Janenschia, HUGE plant-eater

 Kentrosaurus, spiky, armoured plant-eater

 Lambeosaurus, head-crested plant-eater
Leaellynasaura, small, big-eyed plant-eater

Lesothosaurus, small and speedy plant-eater

Lufengosaurus, long-necked plant-eater

 Maiasaura, duck-billed plant-eater
Majungasaurus, large meat-eater

Mamenchisaurus, the plant-eater with the longest known neck!

Massospondylus, plant-eater

Megalosaurus, large meat-eater and the very first dinosaur to be named (even before the term dinosaur)

Megaraptor, large-meat-eater with sickle-shaped foot claw

Microvenator, 'small hunter'... a meat-eater!

Muttaburrasaurus, thumb-spiked plant-eater

 Nodosaurus, large, armoured plant-eater

Notoceratops, horned, frilled plant-eater

 Ornitholestes, small, fast-moving meat-eater with crested nose

Ornithomimus, speedy little omnivore

Othnielia, speedy, two-legged plant-eater

Ouranosaurus, peaked plant-eater with 'sail-ridged' back

Oviraptor, small omnivore (meat- and plant-eater) with parrot-like head

Pachycephalosaurus, head-butting plant-eater

Panoplosaurus, heavily armoured, spiky plant eater

Parasaurolophus, long-crested plant-eater

Pentaceratops, many-horned, big-frilled plant-eater

Plateosaurus, two-legged plant-eater

Polacanthus, armoured, spiky plant-eater

Protarchaeopteryx, feathered meat-eater

Procompsognathus, small meat-eater

Protoceratops, beaked plant-eater

 Quaesitosaurus, large, long-necked, long-tailed plant-eater

 Riojasaurus, an early plant-eater

 Saltopus, small, speedy meat-eater
Saurolophus, duck-billed plant-eater

Saurornithoides, small, fast-moving meat-eater

Sauropelta, well-armoured plant-eater

Scipionyx, small meat-eater

Segisaurus, birdlike meat-eater

Seismosaurus, enormous, long-necked plant-eater

Spinosaurus, hunky, sail-ridged meat-eater

Staurikosaurus, meat-eater and one of the very first dinosaurs

Stegoceras, head-butting plant-eater

Stegosaurus, plate-backed, spiky-tailed plant-eater

Struthiomimus, omnivore (eats meat and plants)

Styracosaurus, multi-horned, frilled meat-eater

Suchomimus, large meat-eater with 'fish-hook' claw

Supersaurus, a long-necked plant-eater, the second-longest known dinosaur

Syntarsus, speedy meat-eater

Thescelosaurus, plant-eater

Torosaurus, three-horned, big-frilled plant-eater

Trachodon, duck-billed plant-eater

Triceratops, another three-horned, big-frilled plant-eater

Troodon, speedy meat-eater

Tuojiangosaurus, armour-plated, spiky-tailed plant-eater

Tyrannosaurus rex, king of the dinosaurs!

Ultrasauros, HUGE dinosaur, this long-necked plant-eater was probably the biggest of them all and very like a *Brachiosaurus*

Unenlagia, bird-like dinosaur, a meat-eater

Utahraptor, fast-moving meat-eater with sickle-like claws

Velociraptor, very fast, very vicious meat-eater

 Walkeria, small meat-eater

Wannanosaurus, thick-skulled plant-eater

 Xiaosaurus, small plant-eater pronounced 'She-oh-sawr-us'

 Yangchuanosaurus, big, hunky meat-eater

 Zigongosaurus, long-necked, long-tailed plant-eater

A BIT ABOUT EVOLUTION

Throughout this book, I talk about animals evolving: reptiles evolving into the first dinosaurs and dinosaurs themselves *evolving* into different shapes and sizes and, ultimately, *evolving* into the first birds. But what is this evolving and how and why does it happen? This is all a part of what we now call 'evolution', an explanation of which was first put forward by the British scientist Charles Darwin.

CREATIONISTS' BELIEFS

Nowadays, most people accept 'Darwinism' as a way of explaining how plants, animals and people have come to be over millions or thousands of years. A notable exception, however, are the Creationists. Creationists believe that Genesis – the first book in the Bible – is the literal truth and that God created the Earth in seven days, and put Adam and Eve in the Garden of Eden, a matter of thousands (rather than millions) of years ago. Creationists believe that dinosaur fossils are the remains of animals that were drowned in the great flood; those which Noah didn't take aboard his ark.

NATURAL SELECTION

'The Creationists' view of how animals and humans came into being used to be the common view. Then, in 1859, Darwin published his *On the Origin of Species by Means of Natural Selection*. The central idea behind this world-changing book was that animals and plants were always evolving – changing – in order to adapt to their surroundings, and those which adapted best survived, whilst those which were slow to adapt died out. This is called 'natural selection' because Nature 'selects' what lives and dies, by how well the animal or plant evolves to adapt.

A CHANGE OF HABITS

Imagine an area with tall trees and low ferns. Here, the long-necked dinosaurs can eat the tree-tops and the smaller dinosaurs, on all-fours, can eat the ferns at ground level. Then, one day, the ferns die out. Perhaps they're destroyed by the ash of a volcanic erruption, and only the trees survive. The long-necks are fine, they can still eat the tree-tops, but the smaller dinosaurs have no ferns and can't reach the trees unless they can pull themselves up onto their back legs and stand on two feet. Imagine a small group of them can do this but, after eating, fall back down onto their four feet to walk on. The more these dinosaurs stand up on their hind legs to eat, the stronger these legs become and when they have

babies, their babies might be born with stronger legs...
Time passes (maybe hundreds, maybe thousands of
years) and these four-legged fern-eaters have evolved,
stage by stage, link by link, generation by generation,
into two-legged tree-eaters. They've adapted. They've
survived. The fern-eaters that couldn't adapt died out
with the ferns a long time ago. This is only a made-up
example – not based on a particular species – remember,
but it gives you an idea of the scheme of things.

THE GENE SCHEME

Darwin's theories caused an uproar, but many people
could see the sense in them except for one important
aspect. How (in my example) could the dinosaurs who'd
developed strong back legs by standing up to feed pass
their strong-back-leggedness onto their offspring? And,
remember, Darwin's theory of natural selection was
supposed to apply to plants too. Today we know the
answer: genes. It is through our parents' genes (whether
we're plant or animal) that we all gain some of their
characteristics.

COMMON MAN!

What really upset the Church at the time, though, was
that Darwin included humans in his theories. He argued
that both humans and apes evolved from the same

common ancestor. (He *never* said that humans evolved from apes, which would have been crazy because it'd have meant that the monkeys at our local zoo might give birth to a human tomorrow!) Christians at the time wanted to see humans as totally separate from the animal kingdom. To suggest that they – *we* – were just another animal was OUTRAGEOUS!!!

A 'YOUNG' PLANET

Today, Darwin's theories are so taken for granted and so accepted as the truth that it's hard to imagine a time when most people thought otherwise. In the early 1800s – 200 or so years ago – in Europe, it was generally accepted that the Earth was just 4,000 – 6,000 years old (based on information contained in the Bible). But, as far back as 1785, a Scotsman called James Hutton argued that there was no way that rivers, lakes and streams could have worn away the landscape the way they had in thousands rather than millions of years. He based this on scientific observations of how slowly water was eroding rock then and there.

ABOARD 'THE BEAGLE'

More and more scientist began to accept that the Earth itself must be older, but surely this had little to do with plants and animals. Then, between 1831 and 1836, the young Charles Darwin travelled on board a ship called *The Beagle*, which was surveying the southern hemisphere. The crew's mission was to make detailed and accurate maps and written and illustrated records of the plants, animals and people they encountered. It was when *The Beagle* reached the Galapagos Islands that Darwin made some very interesting observations.

SUBTLE DIFFERENCES

Here was a group of islands with birds and tortoises on each. At first glance, these animals looked the same. On closer inspection, they were similar but very definitely different. Very soon, Darwin could identify which island a particular bird or tortoise came from, just by studying it... But why-oh-why would each island have its own slightly different set of animals? If God had created all the animals at once, surely He wouldn't have bothered with such tiny, subtle differences, Darwin reasoned. Then he noticed that the environment was slightly different on each island. Some had more trees and less undergrowth than others, for example. Different environments? Different animals? Could one affect the other. Did the animals somehow adapt to suit their surroundings, but how? And it was from these questions that the *On the Origin of Species* grew. Darwin first shared his ideas with the world in a scientific paper that he read out in 1858. This was exactly the same year that another British naturalist, by the name of Alfred Russel Wallace, announced his own theory. Remarkably similar to Darwin's conclusions, Wallace had come up with them entirely on his own.

ALL SHAPES AND SIZES

Evolution and natural selection go a long way to explaining why there was such a weird and wonderful variety of dinosaurs of all shapes and sizes and why some species survived so much longer than others. These were the ones that best-suited their environment, or which could adapt.

GLOSSARY

amphibians – animals that live on land but return to water to breed

bipedal – animals that walk on their two back legs

camouflage – colouring or patterning designed to make animals, in this instance, blend into the background and be less noticeable

carnivore – a meat-eater

cold-blooded – the body temperature of cold-blooded animals change according to the temperature around them. They need the sun's heat, for example, to warm their bodies (See *warm-blooded*)

conifers – trees, such as pine and fir, which bear cones

coprolite – fossilised dinosaur poo

erosion – the wearing away of material (rocks, soil, etc.) by water or wind

evolution – the gradual changing of animals and plants over thousands (or millions) of years in order to adapt to their environment (See *natural selection*)

extinction – the dying out of a species of an animal or plant. For example, the dodo (a big-beaked, flightless, island-dwelling bird) became extinct in the 18th century

foliage – leaves, twigs, branches

fossil – the preserved remains of a once-living thing (See *the answer to Question 18*)

gastroliths – stones swallowed by some plant-eating dinosaurs, designed to help break up the food in the stomach

genus – a group of similar species form a genus. For example, *Tyrannosaurus rex* was a species of the genus *Tyrannosaurus*, which included other similar dinosaurs

geology – the study of rocks

herbivore – plant-eater

mammals – backboned, warm-blooded animals with fur (or hair) which feed their young on milk. Today, they include bats, squirrels, cats and dogs and you and me

meteor – a rock moving through space

meteorite – the remaining part of a meteoroid that has fallen to Earth

meteoroid – a meteor which has passed into the Earth's atmosphere

natural selection – the survival or extinction of animals and plants, depending on whether or not they adapt to their environment through evolution

omnivore – meat- and plant-eater

palaeontologists – people who study fossils

predator – an animal that hunts and kills other animals

prey – the victim (or intended victim) of a predator

radioactive – giving off radiation (strong, usually harmful, rays)

reptiles – cold-blooded, backboned animals with scaly skin. Today, this includes snakes and lizards

sedimentary rock – rock formed from soil and other loose matter being pressed together in layers

sickle – a curved-blade cutting tool

species – a group of animals with common features that can breed with each other

vertebrae – backbone

warm-blooded – the body temperature of warm-blooded animals remains roughly the same, whatever the surroundings. Body heat is gained by turning energy from food into heat. (See *cold-blooded*)

WHERE TO SEE DINOSAURS IN THE UK TODAY

Here are just a few of the places where you can see dinosaur fossils and exhibitions in the United Kingdom — but there are plenty more, so be sure to check your local tourist information centre.

ENGLAND

The Natural History Museum
Cromwell Road
London SW7 5BD

The Dinosaur Museum
Icen Way
Dorchester
Dorset DT1 1EW

Museum of Isle of Wight
Sandown Library
High Street
Sandown
Isle of Wight PO35 8AF

Birmingham Museum
Chamberlain Square
Birmingham
B3 3DH

NORTHERN IRELAND

Ulster Museum
Botanic Gardens
Belfast BT9 5AB

SCOTLAND

National Museums of Scotland
Chambers Street
Edinburgh EH1 1JF

Hunterian Museum
University of Glasgow
University Avenue
Glasgow G12 8QQ

WALES

National Museum of Wales
Cathays Park
Cardiff CF1 3NP

QUICK QUIZ ANSWERS

QUICK QUIZ 1

(a) 'Marvellous' or 'terrible lizard'
(b) Saurischian (lizard-hipped) and ornithischian (bird-hipped)
(c) Madagascar

QUICK QUIZ 2

(a) *Struthiomimus*
(b) Palaeontologists
(c) Camouflage, warning, deflecting/attracting heat, and attracting a mate

QUICK QUIZ 3

(a) There are no such things as flying dinosaurs!
(b) The males have bigger head crests than the females
(c) Australia

QUICK QUIZ 4

(a) Armour, cooling or heating
(b) 1859
(c) Because the teeth reminded him of those of an Iguana lizard
(d) About 14 metres (46 feet)

QUICK QUIZ 5

(a) There's nothing to suggest that one was more successful than the other
(b) From fossilised skin imprints and rare cases of actual fossilised skin (where dinosaur bodies dried out not rotted away)
(c) 'Good mother lizard'. ('Saura' is the female of 'saurus')

QUICK QUIZ 6

(a) Keeping warm and displaying to prospective (possible) mates
(b) Sharks
(c) Pangaea

QUICK QUIZ 7

(a) 'King tyrant lizard'
(b) Cretaceous
(c) Balance

QUICK QUIZ 8

(a) Archosaurs
(b) Carboniferous
(c) Cenozoic

QUICK QUIZ 9

(a) Stratigraphy, reading magnetic signature of rock, radioisotope dating and using index fossils
(b) Preparators
(c) One which eats meat and plants

QUICK QUIZ 10

(a) *Triceratops*
(b) *Pteranodon* (a pterosaur, not a dinosaur)
(c) *Dromaeosaurus*

INDEX